So long as you both shall live

Ed McBain was born in Manhattan, but fled to the Bronx at the age of twelve. He went through elementary and high school in the New York City school system, and the Navy claimed him in 1944. When he returned two years later, he attended Hunter College. After a variety of jobs, he worked for a literary agent, where he learnt about plotting stories and began to write his own. When his agent-boss started selling them regularly to magazines, and sold a mystery novel and a juvenile science-fiction title as well, they both decided that it would be more profitable for him to stay at home and write full time.

Under his own name, Evan Hunter, he is the author of a number of novels, including *Streets of Gold*, *The Blackboard Jungle*, *The Paper Dragon* and *Every Little Crook and Nanny*; as Ed McBain he has written the highly popular '87th Precinct' series of crime novels.

Also by
Ed McBain in Pan Books

Ed McBain

So long as you both shall live

an 87th Precinct mystery

Pan Books London, Sydney and Auckland

First published in Great Britain 1976 by Hamish Hamilton Ltd
This edition published 1978 by Pan Books Ltd,
Cavaye Place, London SW10 9PG
9 8
© HUI Corporation
ISBN 0 330 254408 5
Printed and bound in Great Britain by
Richard Clay (The Chaucer Press) Ltd, Bungay, Suffolk

This is for Jack Scovil

The city in these pages is imaginary.
The people, the places are all fictitious.
Only the police routine is based on
established investigatory techniques.

one

The photographer's name was Alexander Pike, and he was doing the job free of charge because Augusta Blair was a good friend of his and this was Augusta's wedding day. It was also Bart Kling's wedding day, but Pike hadn't met Kling until four this afternoon, shortly before the ceremony — and whereas he naturally wished the groom all sorts of happiness, any real feelings of affection were reserved for Augusta.

Pike had never seen so many cops in his life.

The groom was a cop, of course, a tall blond fellow who seemed a bit bewildered by everything that was going on. This explained why there were so many cops of different stripes and persuasions at the ceremony and now at the reception. All of them were in plainclothes, but Pike would have known what they were even if they'd all come to the wedding naked; he had once done a photographic documentary on law enforcement, and had got to know policemen very well indeed. Actually he liked cops, even if at four o'clock this afternoon one of them had married Augusta Blair, whom Pike had loved with undiminished passion for three and a half years now.

He had met Augusta shortly after she'd come to this city from Seattle, Washington. He'd been at a cocktail party in the Quarter, when suddenly the front door opened, and all conversation stopped. The girl standing in the doorway was tall and slender, with auburn hair that fell loosely to her shoulders. She had high cheekbones, and eyes so intensely green they seemed fierce. Her nose tilted gently away from her mouth, lifting the upper lip slightly, so that her even white teeth were partially exposed. She had good breasts, and long legs, and hips perhaps too wide for fashion modelling, and she moved directly and with swift smiling grace toward a knot of people she recognized. Pike followed her across the room, introduced himself to her, and then took her over to meet Art Cutler, who ran a modelling agency with his wife Leslie. That had been the start of Augusta's career, and also the start of their long friendship.

Pike was now sixty-four years old, happily married and the father of three sons, so presumably his love for Augusta was strictly paternal. And yet, at four o'clock this afternoon he had felt a faint twinge of jealousy when the minister asked, 'Do you, Augusta Blair, take this man to be your lawfully wedded husband?' and then went on to intone the love, honour, and cherish routine and the health, sickness, prosperity, and adversity stuff, ending with the words 'so long as you both shall live?' – and damn if Augusta hadn't answered, 'I do.'

Ah, well.

The wedding reception was being held in a midtown hotel, in what was called its Green Room. Pike would have preferred a better backdrop for his black-and-white photographs, the green being somewhat murky, but he certainly wasn't lacking for subjects. In addition to his darling Augusta and her good-looking (he had to admit) new husband, there were a great many models at the reception, Augusta's friends consisting largely of people in that profession, just as Bart's friends were people in the law-enforcement business. There were other photographers there, too (naturally), all of whom had Nikons slung around their necks, all of whom were taking pictures, but *none* of whom was the *official* photographer. Augusta had asked *Pike* to be the official photographer, and had of course offered to pay him; he had accepted the job joyfully and had refused to accept a dime in recompense.

He didn't know how many rolls he'd exposed during the ceremony itself, but he knew he'd kept the shutter release clicking and the strobe light flashing every few seconds. Most of his angles had favoured Augusta, but that was forgivable. He had taken pictures of Budd standing at the altar (was *that* his name?) with another cop who was his best man, both of them looking up the aisle as though they were expecting an imminent burglary. And he had photographed Augusta's long walk down the aisle on her father's arm, caught every step of it, Augusta looking radiantly ecstatic, her father looking like a paper-mill executive (which was what he was) dressed up in a monkey suit for only the second time in his life, the first time having been his own wedding. Pike had got good reaction

8

shots of the people sitting in pews on either side of the aisle, too, and then he'd caught the anticipatory look on the minister's face, and he'd kept the shutter and the strobe going all through the brief ceremony. Later he'd caught Augusta and Boyd getting out of the limo, and going up the hotel steps, and then he'd got some great shots of the receiving line, and some equally marvellous shots before and during dinner. He was now roaming the room, taking candids of the guests.

The place was packed with dazzlingly beautiful girls who, like Augusta, were used to being photographed, and used to seeing their faces and figures in national magazines, on television screens, and (in the case of at least one girl here today) on motion picture screens. Each knew with unerring accuracy just when to toss her head back, or break into a wide smile, or step out with her skirts flaring, or gesture with her hand, or raise her eyebrows. An instant before Pike pressed the shutter-release button, the pose was struck. A girl could be stuffing an olive into her mouth just before Pike raised the camera to his eye, but by the time he clicked the shutter release, by the time the strobe flashed, she had swallowed the olive whole, lifted her chin, turned her head over her shoulder to give Pike her best profile, and smiled tantalizingly and promisingly into his lens.

He wandered across the room to the bar now, asked the bartender for a bourbon on the rocks, and then sipped at it quietly while he listened to the conversations everywhere around him. Shop talk. Crime and fashion, a great combination for a bleak Sunday in November, your only daughter's wedding day. My only *what*? Pike thought and grinned, and raised his glass in a silent toast.

'It was a medical ad, you see,' a beautiful brunette at his elbow was saying to a husky redheaded cop with a frightening white streak in the hair over his left temple. 'I got to the sitting at three o'clock, and the photographer led me inside, and explained that this was an ad about cancer and about getting checkups and all that, and he asked me if I knew it was a nude sitting. I said, "What do you mean *nude*, what is this?" He said he thought the agency had told me. The idea was the

9

model would be shot nude and the copy would run right across her body, but you'd still of course be able to see her. I told him I didn't do nude work, that I'd rather get shot with a gun than get shot nude, and he said, "Okay then, I guess that's that", and we shook hands and I rode off into the sunset.'

The fellow who'd been Boyd's best man was an Italian detective whose face Pike found interesting. He watched the man now as he danced cheek to cheek with a woman presumably his wife. The man's hair and eyes were brown, the eyes much darker than the hair. The eyes slanted downward, and they combined with rather high cheekbones to give him the look of an amused Oriental. He was a tall man with the easy grace of an athlete, and he held his wife close as they danced toward where Pike was standing at the bar. The wife was extraordinarily beautiful. Black hair, and eyes so brown they appeared black too. She was wearing an off-the-shoulder gown, and as they came closer, Pike saw to his surprise that a small, lacy black butterfly was tattooed on her right shoulder. The man turned to him and smiled lazily, and Pike nodded and smiled back, and then took a picture of them as they danced off to the strains of 'Always', a waltz Pike found sickening but which was played at every wedding he'd ever attended, flying in the face of statistics that promised divorce for one out of every three married couples.

'... I'd ever seen in my life. Tell the girl, Hal. Did you ever see so much blood in your life?'

'That was a lot of blood, miss.'

'Call me Annie.'

'So the minute we saw the blood in the hallway, we drew our revolvers and went tiptoeing into the apartment – am I right, Hal?'

'I *always* tiptoe in. I'm the world's biggest coward.'

'Don't believe him, he's been cited three times for bravery.'

'Who, me?'

'Anyway, we go in there, Miss ...'

'Call me Annie.'

'We go in there, Annie, and guess what?'

'Nobody's in there.'

'That's right. How'd you know that? How'd she know that, Hal?'

'I don't know, Bob. Maybe her father's a cop. Is your father a cop, Annie?'

'My father's a photographer. That's how I *got* in this lousy business.'

Pike sipped at his bourbon and looked across the room to where a detective who'd been one of the ushers was dancing his wife – Pike automatically assumed that any couple over the age of twenty-five *had* to be man and wife – toward the bar. He was easily as tall as the Italian cop who'd been best man, but he was burlier and probably older, unless the baldness was premature. Premature or not, it was the *baldest* baldness Pike had ever seen in his life. Moreover, there was not the slightest trace of five-o'clock shadow on this glistening dome, oh, no. This man did not shave his pate to curry current favour; this man was a natural cue ball. He danced with all the grace of an ox-drawn cart, leading his wife around the floor in something that resembled a cross between a lindy hop and a fox trot, though the band was still playing a waltz. Pike raised his camera and started shooting.

'Are you getting some good pictures, Mr Pike?' the man standing on his right asked. He was a compact man with a craggy nose, iron-grey hair, and flinty blue eyes. Pike guessed he was in his late fifties or early sixties. 'I'm Peter Byrnes,' he said. 'We met earlier. Before the ceremony.'

'Oh, sure,' Pike said, and extended his hand. 'I'm sorry, I've been introduced to so *many* people today ...'

'That's okay,' Byrnes said.

'You're the lieutenant in charge of the squad, right?'

'Right.'

'Right, I remember now.' Pike lifted his glass. 'Here's to the happy couple,' he said.

Byrnes raised his glass, and said, 'Here's to them.'

Both men drank. Byrnes put his glass down on the bar top. Pike put his glass down beside it.

'Never thought I'd see this day,' Byrnes said.

'Me, neither,' Pike said.

'That boy's had more damn trouble with the women in his life . . .'

'What kind of trouble?' Pike asked immediately.

'Well, I don't want to bore you,' Byrnes said. 'I'm just happy he finally—'

'No, go ahead, you won't bore me,' Pike said. He felt a strange sense of foreboding, as though Byrnes would in the next moment tell him something horrible about the man Augusta had married. Trouble with women? What *kind* of trouble? Pike had to know, if only for Augusta's sake, and yet he dreaded hearing the answer.

'This was quite some time ago,' Byrnes said. 'Kling was engaged to a girl named Claire Townsend. They planned on getting married as soon as she'd got her master's. Make a long story short, she got killed in a bookshop up on Culver Avenue. Young girl,' Byrnes said, and shook his head. 'Some crazy bastard came in and shot up the place, killed three other people besides Claire. I didn't think Kling would ever get over it. Took him quite some while.'

'But he *did* get over it, huh?' Pike said, and waited, dreading the worst, and still expecting it. Byrnes lifted his glass and sipped thoughtfully at his drink. Pike waited.

'Didn't go out with *any* girls at all for the longest time,' Byrnes said, and Pike thought, Oh my God, Augusta's married a reformed pansy faggot queer!

'Then,' Byrnes said, 'I forget which case he was investigating, he met this very nice girl named Cindy Forrest, went with her for quite some time. But she broke off with him. Told him she'd fallen in love with a doctor at the hospital where she worked. Just like that. Goodbye, it's been nice knowing you.' Byrnes shook his head again. 'Thing like that can shake a man up all over again.'

'But he's all right now, huh?' Pike prompted.

'Huh?' Byrnes said.

'He *did* finally get over it.'

'Oh, yes, he's fine now. He's got Augusta now,' Byrnes said, and grinned, and raised his glass. 'Here's to both of them,' he said.

'Here's *to* them,' Pike said, enormously relieved.

'I sometimes feel as if that boy's my own son. Both his parents are dead, you know. I sometimes feel he's one of my own.'

'I feel that way about Augusta sometimes,' Pike said.

Both men drank solemnly.

'Is this a wedding or a wake?' someone behind them asked.

Pike turned. It was the Italian cop, Boyd's best man. 'Getting some good pictures, Mr Pike?' he said, and then asked the bartender for a Scotch and soda, and a Canadian on the rocks. 'We met earlier,' he explained. 'Before the ceremony. Carella. Steve Carella.'

'Right,' Pike said, and took the extended hand. 'I'm sorry, I've been introduced to so *many* people today ...'

'Right, right, don't worry about it,' Carella said. 'Why the long face?' he asked Byrnes.

'Weddings make me sad,' Byrnes said.

'Me, too,' Pike said.

'Ceremony,' Byrnes said.

'Ritual,' Pike said.

'You guys sound like Monoghan and Monroe,' Carella said.

'Who's Monoghan and Monroe?' Pike asked, thinking they might be an old vaudeville team. 'Are they an old vaudeville team?' he asked aloud.

'Almost,' Carella said. 'They're Homicide cops.'

'They're pains in the asses,' Byrnes said. 'I don't like Homicide cops.'

'Neither do I,' Carella said.

'Never *have* liked Homicide cops,' Byrnes said.

'Neither have I,' Carella said.

'If you look at it one way ...' Pike said dolefully.

'Huh?' Byrnes said.

'I was saying, if you look at it one way, you could say I'm gaining a cop.'

'Not a *Homicide* cop, I hope,' Carella said.

The band was playing a medley of tunes reminiscent of the forties, and some of the younger models were now trying to dance rock-style to the likes of 'Moonlight Serenade', 'Star Eyes,' and 'I Had the Craziest Dream.' Pike watched the girls and listened to the two cops congratulating themselves on finally getting Kling married off to a 'nice' girl, which Pike felt was a somewhat understated way of describing his darling Augusta. In the next ten minutes half a dozen *other* cops – all in various stages of intoxication – wandered over to the bar to join them, and it suddenly seemed to Pike that someone had called in a 10-13, an 'Assist Officer', and every cop in the vicinity had responded to it. Pike wondered who was watching the store. But one of the cops explained to Pike – had he asked the question out loud? – that there were sixteen men on the squad altogether and that some of them were still back there at the station house taking care of the citizenry, though most of them were right here at old Kling's wedding.

Right on cue, old Kling walked up to the bar in his tuxedo, grinning from ear to ear, a shock of blond hair hanging on his forehead, the victim they'd all been looking for, the cop who'd called in the 10-13. Someone had the wit to say, 'And *here* he is now!' and then all the cops laughed and began slapping him on the back. One of the cops, a man named Andy Parker who looked somewhat dishevelled and unshaven, despite the fact that he was all dressed up for a wedding, warned Kling that in *some* parts of the country – like for example this city – it was a custom for friends of the groom to kidnap the bride on her wedding night, especially if she was someone as beautiful as Augusta. Kling laughed and reminded them all that kidnapping was a Class A felony punishable by life imprisonment, and they all laughed again, and finally Carella shushed them all with the palm of his outstretched hand. Looking around to make sure they all had glasses in their hands (as if they *needed* anything more to drink), he lifted his own glass and said, 'Fellas, I want to tell you how happy this day makes me. I want to say I've been hoping for this day for a long, long time now. Do you remember when this kid first came on the squad, that was after he cracked the Jeannie Paige murder when he was still a patrolman, I think you all remember that.'

There were nods and murmurs of assent, and Hal Willis chose this moment to slap Kling on the back again, and Meyer Meyer winked at him, and then Carella said, 'Well, this kid here has added a lot to that squadroom, we've had a lot of good times together over the years. All I want to do now is wish him the best of good times in the future, the best of everything.' He lifted his glass a trifle higher. 'To Augusta and you,' he said, 'a good marriage, and happiness for years and years to come. Congratulations, Bert.'

That's his goddamn name, Pike thought.

two

'If that guy takes one more picture . . .' Kling said.

'He's doing a conscientious job,' Augusta said.

They had changed into street clothes and were at the front desk of the hotel now, registering for the room they had reserved. Across the lobby, Pike was standing with his camera to his eye, focusing for a long shot of the couple at the desk.

'Does he plan to sleep with us tonight?' Kling asked.

'Who plans on sleeping?' Augusta asked, and smiled slyly.

'I mean—'

'I'll gently suggest that maybe he's taken enough pictures, okay?' Augusta said. 'He's a dear friend, Bert. I don't want to hurt his feelings.'

'Okay.'

'And it *will* be nice to have a record afterwards.'

'Yes, I know. Gus, are you happy?'

'Yes, darling, I'm very happy.'

'It was a real nice wedding, wasn't it?'

'Yes.'

'I mean, the ceremony itself.'

'Yes, darling, I know.'

'There's something awesome about those words,' Kling said. 'When you come to think of it, that's one hell of a frightening contract.'

'Are you frightened?'

'Sure, aren't you? I take this very seriously, Gus.'

'So do I.'

'I mean, I really *do* want it to last so long as we both shall live.'

'I do, too.'

'So ... so let's just make sure it *does* last, Gus.'

'Are you worried about it?'

'No, but – well, yes, in a way. I love you so much, Gus, I just want to do everything I can to make you happy and to see you grow and to—'

'Your key, sir,' the night clerk said.

'Thank you,' Kling said.

'That's room 824, the bellhop will show you up.'

'Thank you,' Kling said again.

Across the lobby, Pike was sitting on one of the sofas, putting a fresh roll of film into his camera. The moment he saw them moving away from the desk, he snapped the back of the camera shut, and rose, and began walking swiftly toward them.

'I just want one more picture,' he said in immediate apology.

'You've really been an angel,' Augusta said. 'Did you get a chance to enjoy the wedding, or were you just working all day long?'

'I had a marvellous time,' he said. 'But I still need another picture.'

'Which one is that?' Kling asked apprehensively.

'I haven't got a single shot of Augusta and me. Bert, I would appreciate it greatly if you took a picture of Augusta and me.'

Kling smiled broadly. 'I'd be happy to,' he said.

'I just put in a fresh roll,' Pike said, and handed Kling the camera and the strobe pack, and then looked around the lobby and manoeuvred Augusta to a potted palm just inside the revolving entrance doors, where a steady trickle of people moved in and out of the hotel. Kling brought the camera to his eye, focusing from a distance of some three feet, and then held up the strobe as though he were the Statue of Liberty. 'Smile,' he said, and pressed the shutter-release button. The shutter clicked, the strobe light flashed. Pike and Augusta blinked.

'That's got it,' Kling said.

'Thank you,' Pike said.

As Kling handed the camera and strobe back to him, he noticed there were tears in Pike's eyes.

'Alex,' he said, 'we can't thank you enough for what you did today.'

'It was my pleasure,' Pike said. He kissed Augusta on the cheek, said, 'Be happy, darlin',' and then turned to Kling and took his hand and said, 'Take good care of her, Bert.'

'I will,' Kling promised.

'Good night then, and the best to both of you,' Pike said, and turned swiftly away.

In the elevator, the bellhop said, 'Are you newlyweds or something?'

'That's right,' Kling said.

'You're the third newlyweds I had today. Is this some kind of special day or something?'

'What do you mean?' Augusta asked.

'Everybody getting married today. Is it a religious holiday or something? What's today, anyway? The ninth, ain't it?'

'Yes.'

'So what's the ninth? Is it something?'

'It's our wedding day,' Augusta said.

'Well, I know that, but it is *something*?'

'That *is* something,' Augusta said.

'Right, I appreciate that,' the bellhop said, 'but you know what I mean, don't you? I'm trying to figure out, is it a day of some special significance where I've already had three couples who got married today, that's what I'm trying to figure out.' They were on the eighth floor now, and walking down the corridor to room 824. When they reached the room, the bellhop put down their bags, and then unlocked the door and stepped aside for them to enter.

In the room, they both fell suddenly silent.

The bellhop wondered aloud why all the double-bedded rooms were always at the end of the hall, but neither of them said a word in answer, and the bellhop speculated that maybe all the hotels were trying to discourage romance, and still they said nothing in response. He put their bags up on the luggage racks, and showed them the bathroom, and the thermostat, and explained how the red light on the phone would indicate there was a message for them, and made himself generally busy and visible while waiting for his tip. And then he did something rare for a bellhop in that city – he touched his fingers to his cap in a sort of salute and silently left the room. Kling put the DO NOT DISTURB sign on the knob and locked the door, and silently he and Augusta hung up their coats, and then began unpacking their bags.

They were neither of them kids. Their silence had nothing to do with virginal apprehension or fears of physical incompatibility or frigidity or impotence or anything even mildly related to sex, which they had been enjoying together and almost incessantly for quite some time now. Instead, their silence was caused by what they both recognized to be a rather serious commitment. They had talked about this peripherally in the lobby, but now they thought about it gravely and solemnly, and decided separately that they'd been speaking the truth when they said they wanted this to last forever. They both knew that no one had forced them into marriage: they could have gone on living together forever. They had each and separately agonized over taking the plunge, in fact, and had each and separately arrived at the same conclusion almost at the same time. When Kling had finally asked her to marry him, Augusta had said yes at once. He'd asked her because he'd decided simply and irrevocably that he wanted to spend the rest of his life with her. And she'd accepted because she'd made the same decision concerning him. They were now married, the man had spoken the words this afternoon at a little past four o'clock, the man had said, 'For as you both have consented in wedlock, and have acknowledged it before this company, I do by virtue of the authority invested in me by the church and the laws of this state now pronounce you husband and wife. And may God bless your union.' The word 'union' had thrilled them both. Union. That was what they wanted their marriage to be, a true union, and that was what each was separately thinking now.

There wasn't much to unpack. They would be here at the hotel only for the night, and would be flying to Guadeloupe in the morning. When Kling finished he asked if he should call down for a nightcap, and Augusta said no, she'd had enough to drink tonight. He asked if she wanted to use the bathroom first, and she said, 'No, go ahead, Bert, I want to lay out some clothes for the morning.' She looked at both her bags then, trying to remember in which one she'd packed what she would be wearing on the plane tomorrow, a perplexed look on her face, her lower lip caught between her teeth as she pondered this very serious and weighty problem.

'I love you,' Kling said suddenly.

She turned to look at him, a slight smile of surprise on her face. 'I love you, too,' she said.

'I mean, I *really* love you.'

'Yes,' she said quietly, and went into his arms and held him close. They stood that way for several moments, locked in silent embrace, not kissing, just standing very close to each other, hugging each other fiercely. Then Augusta looked up into his face, and touched his lips gently with her fingers, and he nodded, and they broke apart. 'Now go take your shower,' Augusta said, and Kling smiled and went into the bathroom, and closed the door behind him. When he came out ten minutes later, Augusta was gone.

He had planned something of a big male *macho* entrance, and he stood now in the bathroom doorway with a towel wrapped around his waist, and saw immediately that she was not in the room, and then saw that the door to the corridor was open. He assumed Augusta had gone out into the corridor for something, perhaps in search of a chambermaid, though he couldn't understand why she hadn't simply picked up the phone if she needed anything. He went to the door and looked out into the corridor, and saw no trace of her. Puzzled, he closed the door to the room and then went to the closet where he'd hung his robe. He didn't expect to find Augusta hiding in there or anything stupid like that; Augusta just wasn't the type to play such childish games. He went to the closet only because he felt suddenly naked with just the towel around his waist, and he wanted to put on his robe. He had begun thinking, in fact, that perhaps the boys of the 87th were up to some mischief. As Parker had explained, a traditional wedding-night prank was to spirit a bride away from her groom and return her later when a ransom was paid, the ransom usually consisting of a nightcap shared with the newlyweds amidst much guffawing and slapping on the back. Kling had never heard of a bride being kidnapped from her honeymoon suite, but the boys of the 87th were professionals, after all, and could be expected to come up with something more inventive than simply snatching a girl from a wedding reception. As Kling grabbed the knob on the closet door, it all began to seem not only possible but likely. They had undoubtedly found out which room Kling and Augusta were in, and then either loided the door lock with the plastic DO NOT DISTURB sign, or actually used a pick and tension bar on it, cops being just as good as burglars when it came to such matters. Wearily he opened the closet door. He liked the guys on the squad a lot, but he and Augusta had to get up early in the morning to catch their plane, and he considered the prank not only foolish but inconsiderate as well. As he reached for his robe he realized that he'd now have to sit around here twiddling his thumbs till those crazy bastards decided to call with their ransom demand. And then, when they finally *did* bring Augusta back, there'd be another half-hour of drinking and laughing before he finally got rid of them. He noticed then that Augusta's overcoat was still on the clothes bar, just where she'd hung it when they first entered the room.

He was still not alarmed – but a quiet, reasoning, deductive part of his mind told him that this was November and the temperature outside was somewhere in the low thirties, and whereas the boys of the 87th might be spirited, they certainly weren't stupid or cruel; they would never have taken

Augusta out of the hotel without a coat. Well, now, wait a minute, he thought. Who says they had to take her out of the hotel? They may be sitting in the lobby, or better yet, the bar right this very minute, having a few drinks with her, laughing it up while they watch the clock till it's time to call me. Very funny, he thought. You've got some sense of humour, fellows. He went to the phone, picked up the receiver, and then sat on the edge of the bed while he dialled the front desk. He told the clerk who answered that this was Mr Kling in 824, he'd just checked in with his wife, a tall girl with auburn hair...

'Yes, sir, I remember,' the clerk said.

'You don't see her anywhere in the lobby, do you?' Kling asked.

'Sir?'

'My wife, Mrs Kling. She isn't down there in the lobby, is she?'

'I don't see her anywhere in the lobby, sir,'

'We were expecting some friends, you see, and I thought she might have gone down to meet them.'

'No, sir, she's not in the lobby.'

'*Would* you have seen her if she'd come down to the lobby?'

'Well, yes, sir, I suppose so. The elevators are just opposite the desk, I suppose I would have seen her if she'd taken the elevator down.'

'What about the fire stairs? Suppose she'd taken those down?'

'The fire stairs are at the rear of the building, sir. No, I wouldn't have seen her if she'd taken those down. Unless she crossed the lobby to leave the building.'

'Any other way to leave the building?' Kling asked.

'Well, yes, there's the service entrance.'

'Fire stairs come anywhere near that?'

'Yes, sir, they feed into both the lobby *and* the service courtyard.'

'What floor's the bar on?'

'The lobby floor, sir.'

'Can you see the bar from the front desk?'

'No, sir. It's at the other end of the lobby. Opposite the fire stairs.'

'Thank you,' Kling said, and hung up, and immediately dialled the bar. He described Augusta to the bartender and said she might be sitting there with some fellows who looked like detectives. He was a detective himself, he explained, and these friends of his, these colleagues, might be playing a joke on him, this being his wedding night and all. So would the bartender please take a look around and see if they were down there with his wife? 'And, listen, if they *are* there, don't say a word to them, okay?'

'I don't *have* to take a look around, sir,' the bartender said. 'There're only two people in here, and they're both old men, and they don't look nothing like what you described your wife to me.'

'Okay,' Kling said.

'They kidnapped *my* wife on our wedding night, too,' the bartender said drily. 'I wish now they woulda kept her.'

'Well, thanks a lot,' Kling said, and hung up.

It was then that he saw Augusta's shoe. Just the one shoe. Lying alongside the wastebasket on the floor there. Near the dresser. Just to the left of the door, near one of the dressers. The pair she'd put on when she changed out of her bridal costume. But no longer a pair. Just one of them. One high-heeled pump lying on its side near the wastebasket. He went to it and picked it up. As he looked at the shoe (telling himself there was still no reason to become alarmed, this was just a prank, this *had* to be just a prank) he was suddenly aware of a cloying scent that seemed to be coming from the wastebasket at his feet. He put the shoe on the dresser top, and then knelt and looked into the wastebasket. The aroma was sickeningly sweet. He immediately turned his head away, but not before he'd seen a large wad of absorbent cotton on the bottom of the otherwise empty basket. He realized at once that the smell was emanating from the cotton, and suddenly recognized it for what it was: chloroform.

It was then that he became alarmed.

three

Steve Carella arrived at the hotel at precisely ten minutes past midnight to find Kling in a state that could generously be described only as hysteria. He was smoking when he let Carella into the room, something Carella had never seen him do in all the years they'd been working together. He closed the door behind Carella and immediately began pacing the room. He was wearing tan gabardine slacks, blue sports shirt open at the throat, a tan cardigan sweater over it, tan socks, brown loafers. He looked like a gentleman horse breeder, dressed casually for a day at the races, lacking only a pair of binoculars slung around his neck. But his nervous pacing seemed more suited to the maternity ward of a hospital. Carella immediately told him to *sit* down and *calm* down. Kling did neither.

'Have you called anyone but me?' Carella asked.

'No. I figured if there's going to be a ransom demand—'

'Right ...'

'—first thing they'll say is "Don't call the police." —Shit, Steve, I *am* the police! Who'd be crazy enough to pull a stupid fucking thing like this?'

His use of profanity, too, was unusual. He was puffing and pacing, and swearing like a sailor, and there was a feverish glow on his face, and his eyes seemed moist and on the edge of tears.

'All right, calm down now,' Carella said. 'Let's try to work up a timetable, okay? Tell me when you left the room.'

'I went into the bathroom at about eleven-twenty, and came out about eleven-thirty.'

'Hear anything during that time? Any sounds of a struggle, any—'

'Nothing. I was in the *shower*, Steve. How could I hear—'

'You weren't in the shower all that time, were you? You came *out* of the shower at some point, and you dried yourself, didn't you? I'm assuming you dried yourself, Bert.'

'Yes. I also brushed my teeth.'

23

'*After* you got out of the shower?'

'Yes.'

'All right, did you hear anything while you were drying yourself or brushing your teeth?'

'Nothing.'

'How long were you in the shower?'

'About five minutes.'

'Then whoever abducted Augusta—'

'Christ!' Kling said.

'What's the matter?'

'The one fucking thing I don't need right now is *cop* talk!'

'All right, fine. Whoever *took* Augusta out of this room did it during the five minutes you were actually in the shower. Sometime between eleven-twenty and eleven-twenty-five.'

'Yes. Steve, can we just—'

'Take it easy,' Carella said. 'Were you and Augusta talking before you left the room?'

'Talking? I guess so. No, wait a minute, we weren't. Well, we exchanged a few words. But we were pretty quiet, I guess.'

'When did you exchange the few words?'

'I asked her if she wanted a nightcap.'

'Uh-huh,' Carella said, and nodded.

'And she said she'd had too much to drink already.'

'Uh-huh, was that it?'

'No, then she, uh ... no, *I* asked *her* if she wanted to use the bathroom first, and she said she wanted to lay out the clothes she'd be wearing in the morning, and then, uh, I told her I loved her.'

'Uh-huh, uh-huh.'

'And, uh, she said she loved me, too, I guess, and we, uh, embraced, and then I went into the bathroom to shower.'

'Did she say anything to you before you went into the bathroom?'

'Yeah. She said, "Now go and take your shower."'

'So if someone had been listening outside the door, he'd have known you were leaving the room at that point.'

'I guess so.'

'Especially if he didn't hear any voices after that.'

'Yeah.'

'Have you left this room since you called me?'

'No.'

'You didn't check out the fire stairs or anything?'

'No.'

'Did you talk to anyone in the hotel? Elevator operators, anyone who might have seen her or the person who—'

'I spoke to the desk clerk and also the bartender. This was when I thought you guys were kidding around.'

'What do you mean?'

'What Parker said at the reception. About brides being kidnapped on their wedding night. I thought maybe ...'

'Yeah, well, mmm,' Carella said, and grimaced. 'Have you talked to anyone else here at the hotel? Aside from the desk clerk and the bartender?'

'No.'

'How do you feel?'

'Okay.'

'Bert, I want you to stay out of this one.'

'Why?'

'I want you to relax a bit.'

'I'm relaxed,' Kling said.

'You don't look that way to me. When they call here, they're going to ask to talk to you. You've got to stay on top of this, Bert, so you can stall them while we—'

'I *am* on top of it! If you'd just stop the bullshit and—'

'Bert,' Carella said very quietly. 'Come on, huh?'

Kling said nothing.

'Let us handle it, okay? Just put yourself out of it for now. Your only job is to talk to those people when they call.'

Kling still said nothing.

'Bert? Do you hear me?'

'Yes.'

'Okay then.'

'What do they hope to get from a salaried cop?' Kling asked. He did not expect an answer; he was shaking his head and staring down at his own shoes.

'Has her father got money?' Carella asked.

'I suppose so. He owns a paper mill in Seattle.'

'Then maybe he's the target,' Carella said. He thought about this for a moment, nodded his head in the equivalent of a shrug, and then went to the telephone to make his various calls. When he got off the phone, he saw Kling reaching into Augusta's bag for another cigarette.

'You don't need that,' he told him.

'I need it,' Kling said.

Carella nodded again, but this time the nod was more like a sigh. 'Tech crew should be here within ten minutes, the lieutenant and Meyer are on their way, too. We want to cool this for now, Bert, keep the hotel people in the dark as long as we can. At least until we've had some contact. Okay?'

'Yeah,' Kling said glumly.

'I want to check out those fire stairs. Will you be all right?'

'Yeah.'

'Bert?'

'Yeah, yeah.'

'Okay,' Carella said, and went out of the room.

The main entrance to the hotel was on Mayr Terrace, and the fire stairs were at the rear of the building, opening on a service courtyard between the hotel and the apartment house adjacent to it. Carella, reasoning that anyone carrying an unconscious woman would hardly take her down in the elevator, automatically tried the fire stairs as the most logical escape route. The room from which Augusta had been abducted was on the eighth floor of the hotel, and there were seventeen floors in all. Carella had a choice of moving either up or down – Augusta's kidnapper could have headed for the service court below or the roof above. Again, remembering that the kidnapper had been carrying the dead weight of an unconscious woman, Carella reasoned he'd have taken the easiest path of escape – to the service court below. He started down the steps.

On the third-floor landing, he found Augusta's second shoe. It had probably fallen from her foot as the kidnapper moved downstairs with his heavy burden. Carella put the shoe into his coat pocket and continued down to the lobby floor. There were two fire doors on the landing there. One of them opened onto the lobby; the other opened onto the courtyard outside. He knew the kidnapper would not have carried Augusta across the lobby, so he opened the door to the courtyard. A fierce November gust of wind whipped into the building, causing his coat to flap wildly about his legs. He went out into the courtyard, his hair blowing, his eyes at once beginning to tear. Immediately opposite the exit door, some thirty feet from the hotel, there was the unbroken brick wall of the apartment house next door. On Carella's left, as he stood with his back to the exit door, he could see the driveway that ran between the two buildings, and he could see the early-morning traffic on the cross street. On his right he saw a bank of grimy windows running like a lighted bridge from hotel to apartment house, part of a low stucco structure that crouched between the two buildings as though frightened it would be squashed flat by one or other of them. A metal door to the right of the windows was painted red. Carella did not appreciate the current slang for cops, but neither had he appreciated the terminology that was in vogue when he'd first made detective. In those days, detectives were called 'bulls'. Nonetheless, he zeroed in on that red door as if it were a cape being waved by a matador. Crossing the windy courtyard, cursing the cold, he reached the door and knocked on it.

There was no answer.

He knocked again.

'Who is it?' a voice said.

'Police,' Carella said.

'*Who?*'

'Police officer. Would you please open the door, sir?'

'Just a second, okay?'

The man who unlocked and then opened the door appeared to be in his early seventies, a tall thin man wearing eyeglasses, black trousers, a white shirt, and a long dirty white apron. He was holding a broom in his left hand.

'Could I see your badge, please?' he asked Carella.

Carella showed him the gold shield.

'Come in, Officer,' the man said, and then waited for Carella to enter, and closed and locked the door behind him. As soon as he had performed this task, he shifted the broom to his right hand. 'Cold out there, ain't it?' he said.

'Very,' Carella said.

The man had brown eyes, magnified by the thick lenses of his glasses. He had a very soft speaking voice, so low that Carella had trouble hearing him. A grey bristle was on his chin and cheeks. 'What's the trouble, Officer?' he asked.

'This is a routine investigation,' Carella said, hauling out the old police pacifier. Routine investigation. Two words that usually satisfied any honest citizen's curiosity. Try them on a crook, though, and they often struck terror in his heart. 'How long have you been in here tonight, sir?'

'I got in around ten.'

Looking around now, Carella saw that he was in a kitchen. A huge black cookstove ran almost the length of the courtyard wall. The grimy windows Carella had seen from outside had undoubtedly got that way from the grease spatters of the day's cooking. There was a large butcher-block worktable opposite the stove, spotless stainless-steel bowls and utensils ranged on it in readiness for the morning's work. On the other side of the worktable, there was a bank of stainless-steel refrigerators. 'Is this a restaurant?' Carella asked.

'Luncheonette,' the old man answered. 'The R & M Luncheonette. I seen you looking at the windows there. Haven't got to them yet. They'll be spotless clean, time I leave here.'

'You say you got to work at ten?' Carella asked.

'That's right. My job's cleaning up. They close right after supper, usually around nine o'clock, sometimes a little later. I come in at ten. My name's Bill Bailey, please don't make no jokes, okay? Every time I meet somebody, he says, "Bill Bailey, whyn't you go on home and stop causing that woman so much trouble?"' Bailey chuckled and shook his head. 'Wish they'd never written that song, I've got to tell you.' But it was plain to see he enjoyed whatever small notoriety the song offered him. 'What's *your* name, sir, if I may ask?'

'Detective Carella.'

'How do you do, sir?' Bailey said, and shifted the broom to his left hand again, and extended his right hand.

'How do you do?' Carella said. They shook hands almost solemnly. For Bailey, this must have been a rare occurrence, a detective coming into the luncheonette in the early hours of the morning. He lingered over the handshake, savouring it, and finally let Carella's hand go.

'Mr Bailey?' Carella said.

'Yes, sir?'

'I wonder if you can tell me whether you saw anyone outside in the courtyard tonight?'

'A person, do you mean?'

'Yes. A person.'

'No, sir, I did not see any person out there.'

'What *did* you see?' Carella asked, suddenly realizing that Bailey had wanted clarification only because he'd seen something *other* than a person.

'A truck,' Bailey said.

'When was this?'

'Pulled in around eleven o'clock, I would say. Around that time.'

'What kind of a truck?'

'A white one. Driver backed it in. Backed it all the way up the alley to where the hotel's fire door is. You don't see many of the delivery trucks doing that. Fellows usually drive them in headfirst, and then back them out when they're leaving. This fellow backed it in all the way.'

'How'd you happen to see it?' Carella asked. 'Were you outside in the courtyard?'

'In this weather? No, *sir*,' Bailey said. 'I saw it through the windows there.' He gestured with the broom toward the grease-stained windows over the stove. The windows were set about five feet above the floor. Bailey was a thin scarecrow of a man, tall enough to have seen through the windows easily – if they'd been clean. But looking through them now, Carella had the feeling that a veil had been dropped over his eyes. He could barely make out the brick wall of the apartment building on the right, and could certainly not see the fire door of the hotel on the left.

'You saw the truck through these windows, huh?' Carella said.

'Yes, sir, I did. I know what you're thinking, sir. You're thinking I'm an old man wearing these thick eyeglasses here, and those windows are filthy, so how could I see anything out there in the courtyard? Well, sir, the windows *are* filthy, that's true, but I'm *used* to looking through them that way, and I see all *sorts* of things out there, especially in the summertime when sometimes the chambermaids are out there with the bell-hops. Not in the winter, mind you. Too cold. Freeze their behinds off out there. The thing people usually forget about anybody who wears eyeglasses, no matter *how* thick those glasses may be, is that the glasses are there to *correct* the person's vision, do you understand? Man can see just fine when he's got his glasses on. It's only when he takes them *off*, he can't see too well.'

'What kind of a truck did you say it was?' Carella asked.

'A white one. Must've been a milk truck, don't you think? Or a bakery truck.'

'Would they normally make deliveries at eleven o'clock?' Carella asked.

'No, that's right, they usually don't, leastways I've never seen them. Maybe it was a linen truck. I would guess the hotel gets lots of linens picked up and delivered, wouldn't you guess?'

'Mr Bailey, you didn't see any lettering on the truck, did you?'

'No, sir. I only saw the back of the truck. It backed in. Stopped near the fire door there.'

'And you didn't see anyone getting out of the truck.'

'No, sir. I just looked out when I heard the truck, and then I went back to my work. I thought at first it might've been a delivery for *us*, you see, and I was worried about what to do, since they don't give me no money to pay for deliveries, and besides, I've never had one at night all the time I've been working here. But nobody knocked on the door, so I figured it wasn't for us. Tell you the truth, when *you* knocked on the door, I thought that might be a delivery, too.'

'When did the truck leave, Mr Bailey, can you tell me that?'

'Must've been about eleven-thirty. I didn't *see* it leaving, mind you, but I heard it, and I looked up at the clock. It was just about eleven-thirty, give or take.'

'Well, thanks a lot, Mr Bailey, you've been very helpful.'

'Want a cup of coffee? I've got a pot right here on the stove.'

'Thank you, no, I've got to be going.'

'Nice talking to you,' Bailey said, and unlocked the door for him. Carella stepped out into the courtyard again. The wind was vicious; it ripped through the cloth of his coat and gnawed his bones to the marrow. Newspapers flew about the courtyard like winged night marauders, flapping noisily in the air, slapping blindly against the surrounding brick walls. He walked to the fire door and tried to open it, but it was blindlocked on the courtyard side. Ducking his chin into his collar, he thrust his hands into his pockets and walked up the driveway, and out onto the sidewalk and up the block, and around the corner to the front entrance of the hotel.

four

They had set the police machinery in motion, and now they sat down to wait in the early hours of the morning, the empty hours of the night. It was Monday already, November the tenth, but it still felt like Sunday night. Contrary to Carella's hopes, it had proved impossible to keep the hotel staff from knowing what had happened. Too many technicians were crawling all over the room, the corridor, the elevator, the fire stairs, and the service courtyard, installing equipment and searching for fingerprints, footprints, and tyre tracks. In the end Carella simply warned the hotel staff that the newspapers were not to get hold of this story, and he hinted broadly that news of an abduction wouldn't do much to help the hotel's image, either.

A full description of Augusta had been radioed to the police at air terminals, railroad stations, and bus depots, and a teletype had gone out to police departments in all the adjacent states. A police technician and a telephone installer, working in tandem, had hooked the room's phone into a tape recorder, and the phone company had been alerted to expect a possible request for a trace if and when the kidnapper called. There was some question as to whether or not Kling's *home* phone should be similarly wired; it was decided that he'd keep the room at the hotel till sometime tomorrow morning and then go back to his own apartment, by which time the phone there would also be equipped to record. For now, there was nothing more that any of them could do – except analyse what had happened and try to second-guess the kidnapper's next move.

If he was a kidnapper.

Captain Marshall Frick, who was the captain in charge of the entire 87th Precinct, including the uniformed cops, the detectives, and the clerks, seemed to think otherwise. 'It could have been a burglary,' he said. Frick was getting on in years, a man whose thinking was as ancient and as creaky as his white hair prepared one to expect.

'How do you figure a burglary?' Byrnes asked. They were all sitting in the hotel room, waiting for the phone to ring. Kling was sitting on the edge of the bed, nearest to the phone. Meyer was in a chair alongside the recording equipment; he was wearing earphones, one of them on his left ear, the other pushed away from the right ear so he could hear the conversation in the room. Carella was half sitting on, half leaning against the dresser. Frick was in the room's one upholstered chair, and Byrnes was in a chair he'd pulled out from the desk. 'With all due respect, Marshall, why would a burglar have come in here with chloroform?'

'I know burglars who've used chloroform,' Frick said. 'I've even known burglars who brought steaks with them, to feed to the watchdog.'

'Yes – but, Captain,' Carella said, 'nothing was stolen from the room.'

'He may have been scared off,' Frick said.

'By what?' Carella asked, and belatedly added, 'Sir?'

'By the girl herself,' Frick said. 'Kling says he went in the bathroom to shower, which means that anybody standing outside the door there, listening, wouldn't have heard anyone talking in the room, might have thought the room was empty. He picked the lock—'

'No pick marks on the lock, Marshall,' Byrnes said.

'All right, then, he *loided* it. Or maybe he used a key, who the hell knows? Some hotels, you can walk right up to the desk, ask for a key to a certain room, they'll hand it to you without even asking you your name. That could have happened here. In any case, how*ever* he got in, he was surprised to find the room occupied. So he hit the girl with chloroform and dragged her out of the room with him.'

'Why, sir?' Carella said.

'Because she got a good look at him, that's why,' Frick said.

'You think he had the chloroform all ready when he came in, is that it?'

'That could be it, yes.'

'Even though he expected the room to be empty?'

'Yes, it's possible,' Frick said. 'It's possible it could have happened that way.'

'Marshall, this looks like a kidnapping to me,' Byrnes said. 'I honestly don't think we're dealing with a burglary here.'

'Then where's the ransom call?' Frick asked. 'It's four o'clock in the morning, the girl was taken out of here at eleven-thirty, where's the call?'

'It'll come,' Byrnes said.

'I'd be checking out my hotel burglars if this was my case. I'd be finding out which of the hotel burglars have been active in the midtown area in recent months. And which of them have used chloroform as part of their MO.'

'Marshall, with all due respect,' Byrnes said, 'I have never in all my years on the force heard of a burglar who used chloroform as part of his regular working MO. Steaks to dogs, yes. Hamburger, even. *That* I've heard of. But I've never heard of a burglar going in with chloroform.'

'I've heard of it,' Frick insisted.

'Where?' Byrnes asked.

'When I was working in Philadelphia.'

'Well, anything can happen in Philadelphia.'

'Yes, and frequently does,' Frick said.

'But this looks like a bona-fide kidnapping to me,' Byrnes said, 'and I've instructed the squad to investigate it as such.'

'It's your squad, you handle it as you see fit,' Frick said. 'I was merely offering an opinion.'

'Thank you, Marshall. I assure you it was appreciated.'

'Don't mention it,' Frick said.

Listening, Kling thought Frick ought to be retired. Or embalmed. The man sounded like a hairbag riding shotgun in an RMP car instead of a man in command of a precinct. The captain was off on another tack now; apparently convinced at last that burglary had not been the motive here, he was relating an absurd kidnapping story.

'I once had a case in Philadelphia,' he said, 'where a man kidnapped his own wife in an attempt to extort money from his father-in-law. Damndest thing I ever did see. We were working on it for three days and three nights before we tipped to the fact that—'

'Sir,' Carella interrupted, 'I wonder if we might ask Kling some questions.'

'Eh?' Frick said.

'Because it occurred to me, sir, that being as close to this as we all are, we might be in danger of ignoring procedure we'd normally—'

'Well, of course, do what you *want* to do,' Frick said, but his tone was injured and he immediately began to sulk.

'Bert, we *know* you, but we *don't* know you,' Carella said.

'We've been operating on the assumption that nobody in his right mind would expect any kind of decent ransom from a salaried cop; we've been thinking Augusta's father was the target. Okay, here's what I want to ask you. *Do* you have any money socked away we wouldn't know about? Anything that would make a kidnapper—'

'We've got three thousand dollars in the bank,' Kling said. 'It's a joint account, and it's what we had left after we furnished the new apartment.'

'There's the possibility, though,' Meyer said, 'that somebody might have got it in his head Augusta was rich, you follow me? Because she's a high-priced model and all.'

'Yeah, we ought to consider that,' Byrnes admitted.

'Bert, I want to ask you the questions I'd normally ask anybody, okay?' Carella said. 'Forgetting you're an experienced detective for the moment, okay? You've probably asked yourself these same questions, but let me ask them out loud, okay?'

'Go ahead,' Kling said. He glanced at Captain Frick, who was sitting in the armchair, plainly miffed, a scowl on his face, his hands clasped over his expansive middle. The hell with *you*, Kling thought. She's *my* wife.

'First, Bert, have you or Augusta received any threatening telephone calls or letters within recent weeks?'

'No.'

'Was there anyone at the agency ... that's the Cutler Agency, isn't it?'

'Yes,' Kling said.

'That's the biggest modelling agency in the city,' Byrnes said to Frick in an attempt to mollify him. Frick merely nodded curtly.

'Was there anyone at the agency,' Carella went on, 'any of the other girls, or even the Cutlers themselves, who for one reason or another might have had something against Augusta? Anything like professional rivalry or jealousy or whatever the hell? Was she getting more bookings than the other girls, for example? Or, I don't know, did she land a big account somebody else was after? You'd know about these things better than we would, Bert, you probably talked about her job, didn't you? *Was* there anything like that you can think of?'

'No,' Kling said. 'You know her, Steve, she's really a terrific girl, everybody likes her. That sounds like I'm blowing my own horn, I know, but—'

'No, no.'

'—really, it's the truth.'

'You've got me thinking,' Meyer said.

'Yeah?'

'Suppose this is somebody who's got a grudge against *Bert*. Never mind Augusta. Suppose this is somebody getting back at *Bert*.'

'Boy, *that* opens a can of peas,' Byrnes said.

'For an arrest, do you mean?' Frick asked suddenly.

'What?' Meyer said.

'Getting back at him for an arrest he made?'

'Yes, sir. That's what I had in mind.'

'That's a distinct possibility,' Frick said, nodding, his hands still folded over his middle. 'I know of many cases where a policeman or his family were threatened or actually harmed after an arrest had been made. That's a good thought. Pete, if I may intrude . . .'

'Go ahead, Marshall.'

'I'd like to suggest that you put a man to work checking on Kling's arrest record. Find out who's still in jail, who's been released, and so on. Come up with some names and addresses. I think it's worth a shot. That's a very good thought, Meyer.'

'Thank you, sir,' Meyer said again.

'Very good indeed,' Frick said, and smiled as though he himself had had the idea.

'Bert,' Carella said, 'did you tell anyone at all where you'd be spending the night tonight?'

'No one. Only Augusta and I knew.'

'Then someone must have followed you from the reception. Down to the lobby, I mean.'

'He'd have had to, yes,' Kling said.

'Which means he was at the reception.'

'I suppose so.'

'Can we get a list of all the people you invited to the wedding?' Byrnes asked.

'Yes – but, Lieutenant, there're two hundred people on that list.'

'I realize that.'

'And besides, all of them are friends. I really don't think—'

'You never know,' Frick interrupted. 'With *some* friends, you don't need enemies.' He nodded his head in solemn satisfaction as though he had just uttered an original thought.

'Where is that list?' Byrnes asked.

'In my apartment. The old apartment. We still haven't moved all of the furniture to the new place. The list is in the top drawer of the desk, over the kneehole. The desk is near the windows, on the left as you come in.'

'Have you got a key we can use?'

'Yes, but—'

'I'm not suggesting any of your friends ...'

'We're looking for a place to hang our hats, Bert,' Carella said. 'We don't have to kid you, that's what we're doing.'

'I know, Steve.'

'Because there's not a damn thing to go on yet, Bert. Until that phone rings ...'

'I just thought of something,' Meyer said.

'What's that?' Frick asked, leaning forward suddenly. He had been inordinately impressed with Meyer's earlier thought, which he'd already forgotten, and was now anxious to hear whatever else Meyer might come up with.

'Well, weren't you showing a newspaper clipping around the office a little while ago? An item about the wedding?'

'That's right, I *was*,' Kling said.

'Augusta's picture at the top of the column ...'

'I see where you're going,' Kling said. 'That's right. It announced the wedding, gave the date and the time ...'

'Did it give the name of the church?' Carella asked.

'Yes.'

'So it could have been anybody.'

'Anybody who knows how to read,' Byrnes said.

'Would have known where the wedding was going to take place, could have followed them from the church to the reception, and from there to the lobby.'

'Would have had to ask at the desk, though,' Meyer said.

'For what room they were in, right.'

They were snowballing it now, almost as if Kling were not in the room with them. He had been a part of many similar sessions in the past, but now he watched and listened like a stranger as they concocted a possible scenario for what had happened, and tried to work out an effective plan of action.

'Parked the truck in the service court ...'

'White truck, think we ought to put out an alarm?'

'Could be *any* damn kind of truck. Bailey didn't see the licence-plate number.'

'Amazing he saw the truck at all, way you described those windows.'

'Anyway, that's what he must've done. Parked the truck in the service court, then walked around front to the hotel entrance. Couldn't have come in through that fire door on the court, because it's blindlocked on the outside.'

'Went up to the desk, asked for Mr and Mrs Kling.'

'Or maybe picked up the house phone, got the room number that way.'

'We'd better ask the clerk if he handed out a key after Bert and Augusta checked in.'

'I still want a look at that invitation list, Bert.'

'Be a good idea to get started on those arrest files, too.'

'Want you guys to contact all our stoolies. If this is some kind of dumb revenge thing ...'

'Right, there may be a rumble on it.'

'When's the last time you saw Danny Gimp, Steve?'

'Long time ago.'

'Get onto him. And somebody ought to contact Fats Donner, too. Meyer, you want to sit the wire here?'

'Right, Loot.'

'I'll have someone relieve you at eight. What the hell time is it, anyway?'

38

They all turned toward the windows. A grey dawn was breaking cheerlessly over the rooftops of the city.

She had lost all track of time and did not know how long she'd been conscious; she suspected, though, that hours and hours had passed since the moment he'd clamped the chloroform-soaked piece of cotton over her nose and mouth. She lay on the floor with her wrists bound behind her back, her ankles bound together. Her eyes were closed, she could feel what she supposed were balls of absorbent cotton pressing against the lids, held firmly in place by either adhesive tape or a bandage of some kind. A rag had been stuffed into her mouth (she could taste it, she hoped she would not choke on it), and then a gag, again either adhesive tape or bandage, had been wound over it. She could neither see nor speak, and though she listened intently for the slightest sound, she could hear nothing at all.

She remembered ... he had a scalpel in his right hand. She turned when she heard the hotel door clicking open, and saw him striding toward her across the room, the scalpel glittering in the light of the lamp on the dresser. He was wearing a green surgical mask, and his eyes above the mask scanned the room swiftly as he crossed to where she was already moving from the suitcase toward the bathroom door, intercepting her, grabbing her from behind and pulling her in against him. She opened her mouth to scream, but his left arm was tight around her waist now, and suddenly his right hand, the hand holding the scalpel, moved to her throat, circling up from behind. She felt the blade against her flesh and heard him whisper just the single word 'Silence', and the formative scream became only a terrified whimper drowned by the roar of the shower.

He was pulling her backwards toward the door, and then suddenly he swung her around and shoved her against the wall, the scalpel coming up against her throat again, his left hand reaching into his coat pocket. She saw the wad of absorbent cotton an instant before he clamped it over her nose and mouth. She had detested the stench of chloroform ever since she was six and had her tonsils removed. She twisted her head to escape the smothering aroma, and then felt the scalpel nudging her flesh, insistently reminding her that it was there and that it could cut. She became fearful that if she lost consciousness, she might fall forward onto the sharp blade, and she had tried to keep from becoming dizzy, but the sound of the shower seemed magnified, an ocean surf pounding against some desolate shore, waves crashing and receding in endless repetition, foam bubbles dissolving, and far overhead, so distant it could scarcely be heard, the cry of a gull that might have been only her own strangled scream.

She listened now.

She could hear nothing, she suspected she was alone. But she could not be certain. Behind the blindfold, she began to weep soundlessly.

five

Nobody in the crime-prevention and law-enforcement game likes to admit that informers are a vital part of the setup. There are reasons for this. To begin with, an informer is paid. He is paid cold hard cash. In cases where he is working for the FBI or the Treasury Department or the postal authorities, he is paid very *large* sums of money indeed, and is often protected from arrest and/or prosecution as well. A good informer is sometimes more valuable than a good cop, and there have been cases where a good cop was sold down the river in order to protect a good informer. The money an informer is paid comes from a slush fund, the original source of which is the taxpayer. Whether it is labelled 'Petty Cash' or 'Research' or 'Shrinkage' or 'Mother Leary's Bloomers Fund', the money in that kitty sure as hell does not come out of the pockets of hard-working law-enforcement officers. It is the taxpayer who puts up the scratch, and this is one of the reasons cops, agents, inspectors, and what-have-you are reluctant to discuss their dependency on informers. Taxpayers don't know from informers, you see. Taxpayers only know from rats.

An informer is a rat, and nowhere in the world is a rat appreciated. Taxpayers, therefore, do not feel that rats should be rewarded for their rattiness. Even tiny tots are taught not to respect other tiny tots who are snitches. (It is interesting to note that in the underworld an informer is not known as a 'stool pigeon' or a 'dirty rat', James Cagney notwithstanding. He is known simply and childishly as a 'snitch'.) There is a very stringent underworld code against snitching, and snitches are very often found dead with symbolic markings – such as slashed double crosses – on their cheeks. Fear of reprisal, of course, is one reason why *honest* citizens will not report a witnessed crime to the police. But another reason is the distaste the average, everyday, straight citizen feels toward anyone who would divulge a secret. The secret may very well be the identity of a murderer. Even so, it's not nice to tell. Informers have no such scruples. The only thing *they* worry about is whether or not someone will see them in conversation with a police officer. The cops of the 87th knew the snitching game was a dangerous one, and they were therefore willing to meet their informers better than halfway.

At ten o'clock that Monday morning, Detective Steve Carella sat on a bench in the middle of Grover Park, waiting for Danny Gimp to show up. It was drizzling. The drizzle was cold and wet. Mist rose poetically from rocks and rills. The trees, their limbs and branches bare, stood in gaunt silhouette like slender graveside mourners, the sky behind them a dismal grey. On the road running through the park, there was the sound of automobile tyres hissing on the black asphalt surface. Carella took out his handkerchief, blew his nose, and returned the handkerchief to his coat pocket. His nose was cold. He glanced at his watch. Two minutes had passed since he'd last looked at it. Danny Gimp was usually on time. This morning, though, he had insisted on a fallback. He had told Carella that if he did not meet him at the designated bench by ten-fifteen, he could be found near the statue of General Pershing, on the other side of the park zoo, at precisely eleven o'clock. Carella wondered about this, but Danny would not elucidate on the telephone. It was rare for an informer to insist upon a fallback. The profession had its real risks, true, but it was nonetheless far removed from the more sophisticated world of international espionage.

Danny had arrived at fourteen minutes past ten, just as Carella was ready to abandon the bench. He was wearing a shabby brown overcoat, brown trousers, brown shoes, and white socks. He was carrying a cane, and he was hatless, and Carella noticed for the first time that his hair was getting rather thin. He came limping up to the bench, the limp somehow more marked than it had been the last time they'd talked. There was no nonsense between the two men: they had known each other for a long time, and they had both respected the symbiosis that made their relationship work. They addressed each other on a first-name basis, and they greeted each other like friends who had not seen each other for quite some time. Perhaps they *were* friends. They never much thought about it. In their own minds, they thought of themselves as business associates.

'Some fuckin weather, huh?' Danny said.

'Miserable.'

'How you been, Steve?'

'Okay. And you?'

'The leg bothers me, this kind of weather. I was born too soon, Steve. If there'd been the Salk shots when I was a kid, I never would've got polio, huh?' He shrugged. 'Well, what can you do? I ought to move out to Arizona, someplace like that. This fuckin rain, it really gets in my bones. Anyway, listen, who wants to hear about my misery, huh? What's on your mind, Steve?'

'Why'd you ask for a fallback, Danny?'

'Aw, no reason. I'm just getting cautious in my old age, that's all.'

'Somebody leaning on you?'

'No, no. Well, look, yeah, I'll tell you the truth, there's somebody thinks I did a number on him, and the word is he says he's gonna break my *other* leg if he catches up with me. He thinks I limp cause I had a broken leg once, he don't know it's from polio. The funny thing is I never said a word about this guy to anybody, I swear to God.'

'Who's the guy?' Carella asked.

'His name is Nick Archese, he's a fuckin two-bit gambler, he thinks he's a tough guy. I'll tell you the truth, Steve, you see this cane I'm carrying? You ever see me with a cane before?'

'I don't recall.'

'Well, this cane is new, there's a sword inside it. I mean it. You want to see the sword?'

'No,' Carella said.

'Archese comes after me, or even he sends one of his bums after me, there's gonna be sliced salami on rye, I can tell you. One thing I ain't gonna do is stand still while some bums jump up and down on my bones.'

'You want me to throw a scare at him?'

'How you gonna do that, Steve? You pick him up and muscle him around, he's gonna know I work for you guys, am I right? That'll only make the whole thing worse. Don't worry about it. I can take care of it myself. Only, if you find somebody with a couple of sword holes in him, don't come looking for me, okay?' Danny laughed, and then said, 'So what is it? What can I do for you?'

'Do you know Bert Kling?' Carella asked. 'Have you ever worked with him?'

'Yeah, sure. Tall blond guy?'

'Right. He got married yesterday.'

'Tell him congratulations.'

'Danny, his bride was snatched from their hotel room last night.'

'What do you mean?'

'Just what I'm saying.'

'That's got to be a lunatic,' Danny said. 'Snatch a cop's wife? Got to be out of his mind.'

'Or maybe just angry. We were running through Kling's arrest record early this morning. He sent up too many to count, Danny, we'd be on this all month if we had to track down all the guys who've been paroled and are on the streets again. But two of those guys look like possibilities, and we're anxious to know what they've been up to.'

'What are their names?' Danny asked.

'First one is named Manny Baal. Kling busted him for Robbery Two a long time ago. He drew ten, served the full term, parole constantly denied because he's such a bad apple. When he got convicted, he swore he'd kill Kling one day. Okay, he finally got out of jail last month, and we don't know where he is.'

'Manny Baal, huh?'

'That's his name.'

'How does he spell it?'

'B-a-a-l.'

'What is it – Manuel?'

'No, Manfred.'

'Okay, who's the other guy?'

'The other guy is named Al Brice. Kling busted him on Christmas Eve almost three years ago. He's a possibility, too, Danny.'

'How so?'

'Kling killed his brother.'

'Let me have the details, huh?'

'Kling was dating a girl whose boyfriend was doing time at Castleview. The Brice boys were pals of the con, and they promised to look after the girl while he was away. So they ganged Kling one night and beat him up – broke one of his ribs, in fact. He caught up with them on Christmas Eve. They were running a chicken barbecue joint on the South Side. They put up a struggle when he tried to make the collar, and he had to kill one of them. The other one got sent up for Assault Two, a Class D felony. He drew a fixed sentence of two and a half years because Kling was a cop and judges don't like cops getting their heads beat in. Served his full time, got out this June.'

'And you think he might be gunning for Kling?'

'He's got good reason.'

'Then why go for Kling's wife?'

'Who knows? Danny, we're trying for any kind of lead. So far, we haven't had a peep from whoever's got her.'

'That don't sound like a kidnapping then, does it?'

'Well ... sometimes a ransom demand won't come for days.'

'Mmm,' Danny said. 'How does this guy spell his name?'

'Brice. B-r-i-c-e.'

'Al, you said?'

'Yeah.'

'Is that Alfred or Albert?'

'Albert.'

'Okay, I'll give a listen. Anything else?'

'We need this fast, Danny. So far, we're in the dark.'

'Okay, I'll see what I hear,' Danny said.

'How are you fixed for cash?'

'I could use a double sawbuck, if that ain't pressing you.'

Carella took out his wallet, and handed two ten-dollar bills to Danny. 'About this guy who's leaning on you ...'

'I'll take care of him, don't worry,' Danny said. 'You sure you don't want to see my sword?'

The man Hal Willis went to see was a different kind of informer. His name was Fats Donner. He was a good informer and a terrible man. Willis didn't like him, and neither did any of the other precinct detectives. But he had on occasions too numerous to count provided valuable information, and so he was tolerated. Even his penchant for steam baths was tolerated.

At twelve noon that Monday, Willis found Donner in a sauna *cum* massage parlour on Culver and Tenth. He had been trying to locate him since nine that morning, and had gone to most of the legit emporiums before considering those that mixed steam with sex. For some reason, perhaps because Donner seemed so fanatically religious about losing weight, Willis simply assumed he never would contaminate or confuse his purpose. Sex, even in its handiest form, seemed something that Donner would engage in privately and perversely (his tastes running to rather young girls), and not in a public place where he was hoping to take off pounds.

The name of the joint was the Arabian Nights, and Willis was greeted in the lobby by a muscular black man wearing red velvet trousers, a black velvet vest with gold piping around the armholes, a red felt fez with a dangling tassel, one gold earring piercing his right ear lobe, and a partridge in a pear tree.

'Welcome to the Arabian Nights,' the man said in a heavy Jamaican accent that immediately destroyed any Middle Eastern illusion. 'Would you care to step into the King's Harem, sir?'

Willis showed the man his shield.

The man said, 'This is strictly massage and sauna, nothing else.'

'I'm sure,' Willis said.

'You can spot-check any of the rooms. You find one of our girls engaged in any unprofessional activity—'

'Which profession?' Willis asked.

'I mean it, Officer. We are sincerely clean. Massage and sauna, that is it, mon.'

'I said I believe you. I'm looking for Fats Donner, would you know him?'

'Might he be a huge mountain of a mon?'

'He might.'

'You will find him in the sauna at the end of the hall. I suggest you undress and put on a towel, sir. It can get mighty hot inside there.'

'Thank you, I will.'

'If you'll go through the harem, you'll find lockers just beyond.'

'Thank you,' Willis said.

The harem was draped with a dozen girls of various ages, sizes, shapes, and colours. Half of them were wearing blonde wigs, it being an old wives' tale that men visiting massage parlours preferred blondes. One or two of the girls were actually pretty. They were all wearing transparent houri

46

pants, gold bracelets on their ankles, and black velvet vests similar to the one the black man outside had on. There was nothing but flesh under the open vests. A disparate array of breasts, running the gamut from the insignificant to the profound, greeted Willis as he entered the room and the girls turned to look at him.

'Just passing through,' he said.

'Big spender,' one of the girls said dryly.

He undressed in a room in which there were a dozen lockers without locks. Taking a towel from a neatly folded stack on a shelf opposite the lockers, he wrapped it securely around his waist, and then headed for the sauna at the end of the hall. In one hand he was carrying his wallet and a small leather case containing his shield and his ID card. In the other hand he was carrying his holstered .38-calibre Detective's Special. He felt rather like a horse's ass.

Fats Donner was a great white Buddha of a man sitting in one corner of the wooden sauna, a towel draped loosely over his midsection. His eyes were half closed when Willis came in. He opened his eyes all the way, recognized Willis, and said, 'Close the door, man, you'll let out all the heat.'

Willis closed the door. 'I've been looking all over the goddamn city for you,' he said.

'So you found me, man,' Donner said.

They began talking about Manfred Baal and Albert Brice then.

The man was a Puerto Rican informer who operated a store that sold medicinal herbs, dream books, religious statues, numbers books, tarot cards, and the like. He also sold a wide variety of so-called marital aids, but he kept these in the back room of the shop and showed them only to special customers. His real name, or at least the name he was known by in the *barrio*, was Francisco Palacios, and this was the name lettered in gold leaf on the plate-glass window of his shop. But he was known as 'The Gaucho' or 'The Cowboy' to most of the cops with whom he did business. Only one cop called him 'The Prick', and that was Andy Parker, because once, three years before,

Palacios had come up with some very choice information that would have cracked a big narcotics case and meant a promotion for Parker. But Palacios had refused to deliver the information to Parker because he didn't like him, and had instead given the dope to *another* cop on the squad (Delgado, a Puerto Rican like Palacios himself), for which Palacios would always be 'The Prick' in Andy Parker's eyes and in his lexicon.

The Gaucho looked up as the bell over his door rang. It was raining outside, and he normally did a brisk trade on rainy days. But the man approaching the counter was not a customer. He was a black detective from the 87th Precinct, and his name was Arthur Brown, and The Gaucho had done business with him before.

'Good afternoon, señor,' he said. 'Something I can help you with?'

'Let's go in the back, Cowboy,' Brown said.

In the back room, surrounded by a sophisticated array of dildoes, French ticklers, open-crotch panties, vibrators (eight-inch and ten-inch), leather executioner's masks, chastity belts, whips with leather thongs, and ben-wa balls in both plastic and gold plate, Brown described the two men they were looking for.

The Gaucho nodded, and said, 'I try, eh?'

six

Fat Ollie Weeks came up to the squadroom at two that afternoon.

He was not to be confused with Fats Donner, not that he ever was. When they stood side by side (a proximity neither of the men had ever achieved), one could easily discern a sizeable difference between them: Fat Ollie was fat in the singular; Fats Donner was fat in the plural. There were other differences as well. Fats Donner was an informer, but Fat Ollie Weeks was a detective working out of the Eight-Three. Fats Donner, because he could be found more often than not in the nearest neighbourhood steam bath, was as clean as a whistle and smelled like a freshly bathed baby. Fat Ollie Weeks stank to high heaven, and those who stood close to him sometimes wondered why he did not draw flies. Fats Donner was a tolerant man; his friends over the years had included black girls, Mexican girls, Chinese girls and (on one occasion) a full-blooded Cherokee Indian girl who was fifteen years old. Fat Ollie Weeks was a raging bigot. 'Screw your sister?' he might have remarked to anyone of a duskier shade. 'I won't even drink your water!'

When Carella saw him walking toward the slatted rail divider that separated the squadroom from the corridor outside, he wanted to hide. The squadroom was as open as a flasher's raincoat. Ollie came through the gate in the railing and walked heavily toward Carella's desk, his hand extended.

'Hi there, Steve-a-reeno,' he said, and Carella winced. 'What's this I hear?'

'What do you hear?' Carella asked. Ollie had grasped his hand and was shaking it the way a terrier shakes a rodent. He dropped it suddenly, apparently mistaking it for dead, and immediately pulled a chair out from the desk near Carella's. Drawing it up close to where Carella was sitting, Ollie lowered his voice and said, 'Is it true about this guy Kling?'

'Yes,' Carella said. 'Word travels fast, doesn't it?'

'It's all over the city. If you guys're trying to keep it a secret or something, forget it.'

'Where'd *you* hear it?'

'Desk sergeant gave it to me. I'm gonna tell you something, Steve, case you don't know it. The desk sergeants in this city, they've got like a party line, you understand me? You know, like in those movies about Vermont or New Hampshire, they show everybody gossiping on the party line? That's what it is with the desk sergeants here in this city. A man farts in Midtown East, you can bet they'll hear about it ten minutes later up the Hun' Third in Riverhead. That's the way it works.

Who's this guy Kling, anyway? I don't think I ever met him.'

'He's a good cop,' Carella said simply.

'So he lets somebody steal his wife from right under his nose?' Ollie said, and snorted derogatively. 'What is he, a Jew, this Kling? That sounds Jewish, Kling.'

'No, he's not Jewish.'

'You sure? Some of these kikes, they try to make out they're—'

'Ollie, we have all kinds of people in this squadroom,' Carella said, 'and we don't usually—'

'Oh sure, it takes all kinds,' Ollie said. 'Kikes, spics, niggers ... listen, don't you think I know? We got all kinds up at the Eight-Three, too.'

Carella sighed.

'So what've you got so far?' Ollie asked.

'Nothing.'

'That's what I figured. That's why I come up here, figured I'd lend you guys a hand.'

'Well, we appreciate that, Ollie, but ...'

'What would you guys do without me, huh?' Ollie said, and grinned.

'We've got the thing sort of organized, you know, so ...'

'Yeah, how?'

'What do you mean, how?'

'How have you got it organized?' Ollie said, and then held out his left hand and with his right hand began ticking off points on his fingers. 'Have you got the phone wired, and the phone company alerted? Have you put out bulletins and teletypes to all neighbouring police forces, all airports, railroad stations, and bus depots? Have you checked your files for arrests Kling may have made in the past? Who's still in jail? Who's out on the street? Have you checked whether him or his new wife were fucking around with anybody else on the side? Either of them owe large sums of money to anybody? Any threatening letters or phone calls? Anybody lurking around in recent weeks? Or following either one of them? Anybody at the church or the reception who wasn't invited? Did you do all those things, Steve?'

'Most of them. We know Kling pretty well, so some of them—'

'Yeah, you *think* you know somebody till you open the closet door and find the skeleton hanging there.'

'Well, I can tell you, for example, that Kling wasn't fooling around with anybody. He's a one-woman man, he—'

'How about *her*?'

'Well, I didn't ask him that?'

'So why don't you ask him that?'

'Well, frankly, it would embarrass me to ask him something like that.'

'It wouldn't embarrass me,' Ollie said. 'You want me to ask him?'

'No.'

'It might be important.'

'I don't think Augusta—'

'Is that her name?'

'Augusta, yes.'

'What was her maiden name?'

'Blair.'

'Augusta Blair, right,' Ollie said, and wrote the name down in his little black book. 'Her parents at the wedding?'

'Her father was. Her mother is dead.'

'He live here in this city?'

'Seattle, Washington.'

'Does he know his daughter's been snatched?' Ollie asked, writing.

'Yes.'

'Where's he staying, Steve?'

'At the Hollister.'

'Any ransom demand yet?'

'No.'

'Not to either of them? Kling *or* the old man?'

'Nothing.'

'What time was she snatched?'

'Eleven-thirty last night.'

Ollie looked up at the clock. 'Getting late for a ransom call, ain't it?' he said.

'A little.'

'A *lot*,' Ollie said. 'You wouldn't have a copy of the guest list, would you?'

'Yeah, we picked one up at Kling's apartment.'

'Can you get it Xeroxed for me? How many people were at the reception, anyway?'

'About two hundred.'

'All of them go to the church first?'

'I don't know.'

'Anybody taking pictures?'

'Yes, there were a lot of photographers there. Augusta's a model, she knows—'

'Oh yeah?' Ollie said. 'A model?'

'—knows lots of photographers.'

'Would I know her if I saw her picture?'

'I think so, yes.'

'How about that?' Ollie said. 'Last celebrity case I had was four years ago.'

Carella did not bother mentioning that this was *not* Ollie's case. Instead he said, 'We don't think of Augusta as a celebrity.'

'Oh sure,' Ollie said. 'But you say there were photographers there, huh?'

'Yes. Man taking the official wedding pictures was—'

'Yeah, that's the one I'm looking for.' Ollie wet the tip of his pencil and looked up expectantly.

'His name is Alex Pike.'

'Alexander, would that be?'

'Yes.'

'Alexander Pike,' Ollie said, and wrote down the name. 'You wouldn't have an address for him, would you, Steve?'

'No. He's probably in the book, though. He's a well-known photographer.'

'Alexander Pike, right,' Ollie said. 'You mind if I talk to him?'

'What about?'

'Some of those pictures he took. But first I want a copy of the guest list, okay?'

'Ollie,' Carella said, and leaned over the desk toward him.

'This case is very personal to us, you understand?'

'Oh sure,' Ollie said.

'Things may look pretty calm up here, business as usual, but let me tell you there isn't a man on this squad who isn't sweating. You understand me, Ollie?'

'Oh sure. You don't have to worry, Steve.' He grinned again, and said, 'I'm a good cop, don't you know that?'

Carella *did* know it. He had recognized it reluctantly the last time the 87th worked with Ollie Weeks, and he accepted it as undeniable truth now. Ollie had been of tremendous assistance on an investigation involving both arson and murder, and whereas he was a bigot and a pain in the ass, he was also a very good cop. This contradictory input filled Carella with confusion. It was rather like being asked to forgive Hitler for genocide because he happened to be an excellent public speaker. Well, Carella supposed the analogy wasn't quite *that* strong. Still, he didn't like Ollie, and he felt uncomfortable in his presence. The fact that Ollie seemed to like *him* only made matters worse. Respecting Ollie as a cop, disliking him as a man whose personal beliefs were anathema to everything Carella had come to accept as inviolable tenets, the best Carella could hope for was a quiet disappearing act. No one had invited Ollie downtown to the Eight-Seven, and Carella wished with all his might that Ollie would simply crawl back into the woodwork until such time as he was willing to wash out his socks, his mouth, and his prejudice-riddled head. The one thing Carella did not want was Ollie doing anything that might jeopardize Augusta's safety, or send Kling off the deep end. Kling was barely hanging on, that was the best that could be said for him right now. That telephone in the hotel room hadn't rung since two in the morning, when the installer checked it out to make certain the recorder was working. It was now more than twelve hours later, and Carella was beginning to worry. He did not need Fat Ollie Weeks to compound the anxiety. He decided to put it to him a bit more bluntly. Sock it to him in words even the thickheaded Ollie might understand.

'Ollie,' he said, 'keep out of this case.'

'Huh?' Ollie said, a surprised look on his face. And then he burst out laughing, and said, 'You're hot stuff, Steve, I got to tell you. I almost believed you there for a minute.'

'*Believe* me, Ollie,' Carella said. He was leaning forward, both his arms on the desk top, his eyes level with Ollie's, his eyes refusing to let go of Ollie's. 'Believe me. And stay out of it.'

'I only want to talk to the photographer,' Ollie said, looking injured.

'I'd rather you didn't.'

'Because, you see, if I can get those pictures from him, the ones he took at the wedding and the reception—'

'Ollie ...'

'—and then show them to Kling ... why, we could go down the guest list together, and if there's anybody in the pictures who wasn't on the list ... You see what I mean, Steve?'

Carella was silent for several moments. Then he said, 'Kling might not know everybody on the list. A lot of them were Augusta's friends, he might not have met all of them.'

'Models, you mean? Like that?'

'Yes,' Carella said. 'And photographers. And people from advertising agencies.'

'Like art directors, huh?'

'Yes. And fashion editors.'

'Yeah, I see what you mean,' Ollie said. 'Kling would only know the people from the police department, huh? And their wives, huh? And their girl friends.'

'Yes,' Carella said.

'But *somebody* has to know these other people, no? I mean, besides Augusta. Wouldn't the photographer know them? This Alexander Pike?'

'Maybe,' Carella said. 'Or maybe ...'

'Yeah?'

'Maybe Cutler would be able to identify them for us.'

'Who's Cutler?'

'He runs the modelling agency that represents Augusta.'

'So what do you think?' Ollie asked. 'It's a good idea, ain't it, Steve?'

'It might be worth a shot,' Carella said.

His voice startled her.

She had not known he was in the room until she heard him speak, and she reacted sharply to the sound of his voice, almost as though someone had suddenly slapped her in the dark.

'You must be hungry,' he said. 'It is almost three-thirty.'

She wondered instantly whether it was three-thirty in the morning or three-thirty in the afternoon, and then she wondered how long he had been standing there, watching her silently.

'Are you hungry?' he asked.

There was a faint foreign accent to his speech; she suspected his first language was German. In response to his question, she shook her head from side to side. She was violently hungry, but she dared not eat anything he might offer her.

'Well, then,' he said.

She listened. She could not hear him breathing. She did not know whether he had left the room or not. She waited.

'I will have something to eat,' he said.

Again there was silence. Not a board creaked, not a footfall sounded. She assumed he had left the room, but she did not know for certain. In a while she smelled the aroma of coffee perking. She listened more intently, detected sounds she associated with bacon crisping in a pan, heard a click that might have been a toaster popping, and then a sound she identified positively as that of a refrigerator door being opened and then closed again not a moment later. There was another click, and then a hum, and then a man's voice saying, '... in the low thirties, dropping to below freezing tonight. The present temperature here on Hall Avenue is thirty-four degrees.' There was a brief, static-riddled pause, and then the sound of canned music, and then another click that cut off the music abruptly – he had apparently been hoping to catch the three-thirty news report, had only got the last few seconds of it, and had now turned off the radio. From the kitchen (she assumed it was the kitchen), she heard the sound of cutlery clinking against china. He was eating. She suddenly became furious with him. Struggling against her bonds, she tried to twist free of them. The air in the room was stale, and the cooking smells from the kitchen, so tantalizing a few minutes before, now began to sicken her. She warned herself against becoming nauseated; she did not want to choke on her own vomit. She heard dishes clattering in the kitchen; he was cleaning up after himself. There, yes, the sound of water running. She waited, certain he would come into the room again.

She did not hear his approach. She assumed that he walked lightly and that the apartment or the house or the hotel suite (or whatever it was) had thickly carpeted floors. Again, she did not know how long he'd been standing there. She had heard the water being turned off, and then silence, and now, suddenly, his voice again.

'Are you sure you are not hungry? Well, you will be hungry sooner or later,' he said.

She visualized a smile on his face. She hated him intensely, and could think only that Bert would kill him when he found them. Bert would draw his revolver and shoot the man dead. Lying on her back sightless and speechless, she drew strength from the knowledge that Bert would kill him. But she could not stop trembling because his unseen presence frightened her, and she did not know what he might do next, and she could remember the fanatic intensity in those blue eyes above the green surgical mask, and the speed with which he had crossed the room and put the scalpel to her throat. She kept listening for his breathing. His silence was almost supernatural, he appeared and disappeared as soundlessly as a vampire. Was he still there watching her? Or had he left the room again?

'Would you like to talk?' he said.

She was ready to shake her head; the last thing on earth she wanted was to *talk* to him. But she realized that he would have to remove the gag if he expected her to speak, and once her mouth was free ...

She nodded.

'If you plan to scream ...' he said, and let the warning dangle.

She shook her head in a vigorous lie; she planned to scream the moment he took off the gag.

'I still have the scalpel,' he said. 'Feel?' he said and put the cold blade against her cheek. The touch was sudden and unexpected, and she twisted her head away sharply, but he followed her face with the blade, laying it flat against her cheek and saying again, 'Feel?'

She nodded.

'I do not want to cut you, Augusta. It would be a pity to cut you.'

He knew her name.

'Do you understand, Augusta? I'm going to remove the tape from your mouth now, I'm going to allow you to speak. But if you scream, Augusta, I will use the scalpel not only on the tape, but on you as well. Is that clear?'

She nodded.

'I hope that is clear, Augusta. Sincerely, I do not want to cut you.'

She nodded again.

'Very well, then. But please remember, yes?'

She felt the scalpel sliding under the gag. He twisted the blade and she heard the tape tearing, and suddenly the pressure on her mouth was gone, the tape was cut through, he was ripping the ends of it loose. As he lifted her head and pulled the remainder of the tape free, she spat out the cotton wad that had been in her mouth.

'Now, do not scream,' he said. 'Here. Feel the blade,' he said and put it against her throat. 'That is so you will not scream, Augusta.'

'I won't scream,' she said very softly.

'Ah,' he said. 'That is the first time I hear your voice. It is a lovely voice, Augusta. As lovely as I knew it would be.'

'Who are you?' she asked.

'Ah,' he said.

'Why are you doing this?' she asked. 'My husband's a policeman, do you know that?'

'Yes, I know.'

'A detective.'

'I know.'

'Do you know what happens when a cop or his family are injured or threatened or ... ?'

'Yes, I can imagine. Augusta, you are raising your voice,' he chided, and she felt him increase the pressure against her throat, moving his hand so that *it* and not the scalpel exerted the force, but the gesture nonetheless threatening in that she *knew* what was in his hand, and knew how sharp the instrument was – it had sliced through the tape with a simple twist of the blade.

'I'm sorry,' she said, 'I didn't realize ...'

'Yes, you must be more calm.'

'I'm sorry.'

'Yes,' he said. 'Augusta, I know your husband is a detective, that is what it said in the newspaper article announcing your wedding. Detective Third/Grade Bertram A. Kling. That is his name, is it not?'

'Yes,' Augusta said.

'Yes. Bertram A. Kling. I was very distressed when I read that in the newspaper, Augusta. That was in October, do you remember?'

'Yes,' she said.

'October the fifth. It said you were to be wed the following month. To this man Bertram A. Kling. This policeman. This detective. I was very distressed. I did not know what to do, Augusta. It took me a long while to understand what I must do. Even to yesterday morning, I was not sure I would do it. And then, at the church, I knew it was right what I wished to do. And now you are here. With me. Now you are going to be mine,' he said, and she suddenly realized he was insane.

seven

Alexander Pike thought he had seen enough cops yesterday
to last him an entire lifetime. But another cop was here in his
studio now, and he wasn't even one of the cops who'd been at
the wedding and the reception, and he was asking Pike for
the photographs he'd taken. Pike did not like his looks and
he did not like his manner. He had been photographing beautiful people for more than four decades now, and Oliver Weeks
was definitely not beautiful. Nor was he exactly what Pike
might have called couth.

'We need the pictures you took yesterday, and that's it,'
Ollie said. 'Now, Mr Pike, I been here a half-hour already,
arguing with you, and I'm trying to tell you this is important
to us, and I would like to have the pictures now without
further ado.'

'And I'm telling *you*, Mr Weeks, that all I've got printed
so far are contact sheets—'

'That's fine, I'll take the contact sheets.'

'I'd planned to look them over this afternoon,' Pike said.
'Decide where to crop them ...'

'Mr Pike, you have the negatives, don't you?'

'Yes, but—'

'So make yourself another batch of contacts.'

'Do you know how many rolls of film I shot yesterday?'
Pike asked.

'How many?'

'Thirty rolls of film. That's more than a thousand photographs, Mr Weeks. That's exactly one thousand and eighty
photographs, in fact. It was my plan to look over those pictures
this afternoon ...'

'Yeah, I know,' Ollie said, 'and decide where to crop them.'

'That's right.'

'That can wait, Mr Pike. This is more important.'

'Why? You still haven't told me what's so important about
these pictures.'

'Mr Pike, I am not at liberty to divulge this information,'

Ollie said. Carella had told him that they were trying to keep this whole case hush-hush, at least until they'd heard something from the kidnapper. He had instructed Ollie to get the photographs from Pike without telling Pike what this was all about, a mission Ollie was finding difficult to accomplish. Moreover, Carella's instructions did not make much sense to Ollie. Pike was one of the men he hoped would help match the guest list against the photos. If he couldn't tell Pike what this was all about, then how could he enlist Pike's aid? Besides, Ollie was a Detective First/Grade and Carella was only a Detective Second/Grade, and that meant Ollie outranked him. Still, he didn't like to fly in the face of Carella's instructions, especially since the case was the Eight-Seven's, and also the guys up there were personally involved in it – which was, in fact, a good reason for somebody with a clear head to step in here, somebody who didn't know Kling from a hole in the wall, and couldn't care less about anything but the puzzle of the thing. That was what made police work exciting to Ollie – the puzzle of it. He didn't give a damn about people, dead or alive. All he cared about was the puzzle. He had just told Pike he was not at liberty to discuss why the police felt those photographs were important. He waited now for Pike's answer.

'In that case,' Pike said, 'I am not at liberty to give you these pictures.'

'Then I'll just have to go downtown and get a search warrant, I suppose,' Ollie said and sighed. He had no intention of going downtown to get a search warrant. He was, in fact, trying to figure how he could tell Pike that Augusta had been kidnapped without coming right out and telling him. He would like to be able to say, later, that he had never once mentioned the abduction, that Pike had simply deduced it all by himself. Toward that end, he said, 'You want me to go downtown for a warrant, Mr Pike?'

'Yes, go downtown for one.'

'Mr Pike, I can get one, believe me. I've got pretty good reasonable cause to believe the pictures will constitute evidence of a crime ...'

'What crime?' Pike asked at once.

'Never mind,' Ollie said.

'A crime that took place at Augusta's wedding?'

'Let me put it this way,' Ollie said. 'A crime has been committed, Mr Pike.'

'Where? At the wedding?'

'No, not at the wedding, but shortly after the wedding, and it's possible that the pictures you took yesterday may help us in identifying the persons or persons responsible. Now, that's all I can tell you at this time, Mr Pike, without jeopardizing the victim.'

'Victim? Who?'

'Well, it doesn't matter who. I don't want to jeopardize her by—'

'Her?' Pike asked. 'A woman? Is the victim a woman?'

'Mr Pike, it doesn't *matter* who the victim is. The point is—'

'But is it a woman?'

'Yes, it is a woman.'

'Who?'

'Mr Pike, I'm going to ask you for the last time. If you won't let me have those pictures, I'm just going to have to run downtown and get a warrant, and that'll put a hair across my ass, Mr Pike, it really will. So why don't you cooperate with a hard-working person like yourself, huh, and let me have the fuckin pictures, okay?'

'I'll give them to you if you tell me what happened. Was something stolen from one of Augusta's guests?'

'No, nothing was stolen.'

'Then was someone hurt?'

'No. Nobody was hurt. Not that we know of, anyway.'

'Then *what*?' Pike asked. 'Does Augusta know about this? Does she know you want the pictures?'

'No, she doesn't know we want the pictures.'

'Does she know a crime was committed?'

'Yes. She knows.'

There was something about the way Ollie said, 'Yes,' and paused significantly, and then added, 'She knows,' that immediately told Pike all he had to know.

'Something's happened to Augusta,' Pike said.

'I am not saying anything happened to Augusta,' Ollie said. 'I am not saying anything happened to *anybody*. All I am saying is that a serious crime has been committed, and you can help us a lot by letting us have the contact sheets, and by coming along with me to the hotel, where we can go over them together with Kling and a man you may know named Arthur Cutler, who is probably being telephoned right this minute and being asked to go on down there. What do you say, Mr Pike?'

'If Augusta's in trouble ...'

'Yes or no, Mr Pike?'

'Yes. Of course,' Pike said.

There were, as Pike had promised, exactly 1,080 prints on the black-and-white contact sheets. Moreover, the guest list for the wedding and reception totalled not 200 people, as Kling had estimated, but exactly 212 people. Carella had phoned Cutler and asked him to meet him at the hotel, and then he had called Kling to tell him what he could expect. Kling, who had never met Fat Ollie Weeks, but who had heard a lot about him from Cotton Hawes, immediately asked why he was sticking his two cents into the case. Carella told him that Ollie had come up with a good idea; he added weakly that Ollie was a very good cop, and that they could use all the help they could get. Kling said that according to Hawes, Ollie was a bigoted asshole. Carella told him that was true.

'Then why do we need him?' Kling asked.

'I think he can help us,' Carella said. 'He's got a good head, Bert. He's apt to run things by the book, but occasionally he'll come up with an idea that nobody else thought of. As, for example, the pictures Pike took.'

'Well, okay,' Kling said reluctantly.

'Give him a chance,' Carella said.

'Yeah,' Kling said.

Carella had forgotten to prepare Kling for Ollie's famous W. C. Fields imitation. There were six men in the hotel room now, including Bob O'Brien, who had relieved Meyer and who was monitoring a telephone that defiantly refused to ring. The one time it had rung all afternoon, in fact, had been when Carella phoned not a half-hour ago, to tell Kling they'd be coming over with the photographs and the guest list. It had been silent up to that time, and it had been silent since. O'Brien, sitting on the bed with a pair of pillows propped up behind him, his long legs stretched out, had both earphones on his ears and was reading a paperback book.

The other five men sat on folding chairs the hotel manager had generously provided, around a card table he had also provided. The containers of coffee and the doughnuts on the table had been paid for by the cops. The photographs had been taken, developed, and printed by Alexander Pike. The guest list had been typed four weeks ago by Alf Miscolo in the Clerical Office of the 87th Precinct, as a favour to Kling. The magnifying glass was the property of the 87th Squad, and had been brought to the hotel room by Detective Steve Carella. Art Cutler's clothes were by Cardin, and his hair styling was by Monsieur Henri. That took care of the credits.

As for the photographs, Cutler praised Pike extravagantly for his artistry and sensitivity, and Pike thanked him profusely, and then one or other of the men called off the names of anyone whose picture Carella or Kling did not recognize. Ollie Weeks kept the tally, crossing a name off the guest list whenever someone was identified. By the time they'd looked at all the pictures, they had also crossed off all the names on the list – but they still had pictures of sixteen people who could not be identified by any of them. Ollie insisted that they look at those photographs again. Again, they could not identify them. Ten of the people were men, six were women. It was assumed that some of the unidentified women were wives or girl friends of art directors or photographers who'd been invited by Augusta, and it was similarly assumed that some of the unidentified men were escorts brought along by some of the girls. 'Ah, yes,' Ollie said, using his W. C. Fields voice for the first time and surprising everyone in the room, with the exception of Bob O'Brien, who couldn't hear because of the earphones on his head, and Carella, who'd heard the priceless imitation before.

'What we must do then, m'friends,' he said, continuing with the imitation, 'is go over the list, matching *couples* this time, man and wife, sweethearts and lovers, and so on. Then, whoever's left without a mate, I'll go see them personally and ask them if they know any of these unidentified people. Ah, yes.'

'Ollie, that'll take forever,' Carella said.

'Have we got anything better to do with our time?' Ollie asked in his natural voice, and Kling looked at the silent phone, and then they began going over the list and the photographs yet another time.

The call from Fats Donner was clocked in at the precinct switchboard at precisely ten minutes past four. Hal Willis took the call in the squadroom upstairs.

'Yeah,' he said, 'what've you got?'

'On this Al Brice.'

'Yeah.'

'I know where he is.'

'Where?' Willis asked, and picked up a pencil.

'How much is it worth?'

'How much do you want?' Willis asked.

'I could use a C-note.'

'You've got it,' Willis said.

'I should've asked for more, I got the century so easy,' Donner said.

'Don't press your luck, Fats,' Willis said. 'Where is he?'

'In a fleabag on Fifty-sixth and Hopkins. You want to die laughing? The name of the place is the Royal Arms, how about that?'

'The Royal Arms on Fifty-sixth and Hopkins,' Willis said. 'Is he registered under his own name?'

'Arthur Bradley.'

'You sure it's him?'

'The night clerk knows him. It's Brice, all right. Incidentally, about the night clerk ...'

'Yeah?'

'He don't want trouble later, dig? He done me a favour passing this on.'

'Nobody'll know about it, don't worry.'

'What I'm saying, I don't want Brice to know it was the night clerk fingered him, dig?'

'I've got it. When did he check in?'

'Late last night.'

'What time?'

'Close to midnight, must've been.'

'Was he alone?'

'No. He was with a broad.'

'Did she walk in under her own steam?'

'What do you mean?'

'Was she ambulatory?'

'I still don't get you,' Donner said.

'Did she walk in, or was he carrying her?'

'Carrying her? Why would he be carrying her?'

'Forget it. What's the night clerk's name?'

'Harry Dennis.'

'What time does he go on?'

'He works from eight at night till eight in the morning.'

'Then he wouldn't be there now,' Willis said, looking up at the clock.

'No. You plan to go there now?'

'I think I'll pay the man a visit, yes,' Willis said.

'He's heeled,' Donner said. 'He's heeled very heavy.'

'How heavy?'

'My man saw a .38 in a shoulder holster, and he thinks he spotted a Magnum tucked in Brice's belt.'

'That's heavy, all right,' Willis said appreciatively.

'So that's it,' Donner said. 'About the money ...'

'You'll get it.'

'I'm a little short this week. You think you can send somebody by with it? Like you done before?'

Willis looked up at the clock again. 'It'll have to be when the shift changes,' he said.

'When's that?'

'Midnight.'

'That'll be fine, if you can do it.'

'Sure. I'll have a patrolman drop it in your mailbox.'

'Thanks,' Donner said. 'Listen, this is none of my business, but I wouldn't go calling on Brice all by myself, I was you. From what I hear about him, he's got a very short fuse, and also he'd as soon shoot you as spit on you. Dig?'

'I won't go there alone,' Willis said.

'Not that it's any of my business,' Donner said, and hung up.

Willis went into the lieutenant's office to get the hundred for Donner, and then he typed up an envelope with Donner's name and address on it, and put the money in it, and sealed the envelope. Carella walked in just then, and told him they'd checked and double-checked all the pictures taken at the wedding and reception, and Ollie Weeks was now out trying to run down any strangers in the batch. Willis filled him in on the call from Donner and asked if he wanted to come along when he questioned Brice. Both men went downstairs to the muster room.

At the desk, Willis handed Sergeant Murchison the sealed envelope and asked that a patrolman drop it in Donner's mailbox when the graveyard shift went out. Murchison took the envelope, looked up at the clock, and then asked them where they were going. They told him, and he jotted down the address on a pad alongside the switchboard.

The Royal Arms had never warranted its majestic name, but at one time it had at least been a reasonably habitable hotel. Situated as far uptown as it was, before World War II it had attracted a clientele consisting largely of travelling salesmen seeking clean lodgings at reasonable prices. In 1942, though, much to everyone's surprise, a hotel went up across the street from the Royal Arms. The new hotel was called the Grand, another example of rampant hyperbole. There was speculation

at the time – well, it was actually a great deal more than speculation, since five detectives working out of the Eight-Nine
were busted for taking bribes, and obstructing justice, and the
like. But that was in 1945, long after the Grand had established a reputation for itself and amassed a small fortune for
its owners.

The mob owned the Grand Hotel.

Or so it was rumoured.

This was way back then, Gertie. The mob owned the Grand,
and they had opened it in the asshole end of the city only
because the Hamilton Bridge was on Fifty-sixth and the River
Road, some six blocks north of Hopkins Avenue – and across
that bridge, in the next state, some fifteen miles from the
bridge, to be exact, was an army base full of red-blooded young
American soldiers anxious to get into the city whenever they
got a pass. Not to mention a harbour full of navy ships a bit
farther downtown, full to bursting with crewcut sailors
similarly inclined, though in the navy they call it liberty.
Liberty was what could very definitely be enjoyed at the
Grand Hotel in those dim dear days of World War II. Passes,
too. Both liberty *and* passes could be enjoyed at the Grand.
Furloughs and leaves could be enjoyed there, too. The mob
sure knew how to run one hell of a swinging hotel, especially
when half the detectives of the 89th Squad were being paid
to look the other way. The mob didn't even bother to put
any muscle on the people who owned the Royal Arms across
the street. All the mob did was set up a little night club in
the hotel, to attract the servicemen from hither and yon.

There is nothing illegal about running a night club, not if
you have a cabaret licence, which the mob was able to get very
easily, since the man fronting the operation was as clean as
the day is long. The night club was strictly legitimate. And
where you've got a night club, you've got to expect girls kicking
up their legs on the floor, and girls showing their legs at the
bar, which back in those splendid days of garter belts and
nylon stockings was a sight indeed to behold. You had to
expect such goings-on in a night club; this was, after all, the
big city. So the cops weren't being paid off merely because a few

dozen girls were kicking up their legs at the night-club bar. No, Virginia, the cops were being paid off because a few *hundred* girls were spreading their legs upstairs in the Grand's grandly appointed boudoirs.

The Grand, in short, was what you might call a whorehouse.

And a very successful one indeed, until somebody blew the whistle on all those hard-working detectives who were looking the other way. Meanwhile, the Royal Arms kept sliding downhill because it just couldn't compete with the acres of flesh being offered at the Grand across the street. Eventually, and long before those cops on the pad were caught, even the steady clientele of tired travelling salesmen moved over to the Grand, where rejuvenation could be had for a reasonable price. Ironically, the Grand was now one of those hotels rented by the city for use as a temporary welfare shelter; the people who lived in it were poor, but entirely respectable. It was the Royal Arms that was now a haven for prostitutes and junkies.

Albert Brice was in room 1406 at the Royal Arms.

They asked for him at the desk, and the clerk immediately recognized them as cops and asked in turn how he might possibly assist the police department of this fair city. They told him how.

At seven minutes to five, Detective Hal Willis knocked on the door to room 1406. Carella stood just to his right, his gun drawn. They had talked this one over on the way to the Grand, and had decided to use extreme caution in approaching Al Brice. Normally, knowing the man was armed, they'd have kicked the door in without announcing themselves, and they'd have fanned out into the room hoping to get the drop on Brice before he could use the Magnum. The .38 didn't frighten them much (like hell it didn't), but the Magnum was a weapon to respect. The Magnum could literally tear off a leg or an arm or a goodly portion of the head. They did not want a trigger-happy ex-con cutting loose with a Magnum. They would not have wanted that even if Brice had been alone in the room.

But Brice was not alone. Brice had checked in with a woman at or around midnight last night, a half-hour after Augusta Blair Kling had been abducted from her hotel room. The woman accompanying Brice could have been anyone in the universe, of course; there was no real reason to believe she was Augusta. But Carella and Willis had to operate on the theory that she *was* in fact Augusta, or at least might possibly *be* Augusta. And if the woman in room 1406 was Augusta, the last thing they wanted was a hail of exchanged bullets. So they had asked the desk clerk to call the room and tell Brice the plumber was there to check that faucet, and Brice had said, '*What* faucet? What the hell are you talking about?' and the desk clerk had simply told him he'd send the plumber right up. Had the Royal Arms been a fancier hotel, Willis might have pretended he was a bellhop. The truth of the matter, though – sad to relate – was that the Royal Arms didn't *have* a bellhop, and so Willis knocked on the door, and when Brice called, 'Who is it?' Willis said, 'The plumber.'

'I didn't ask for no plumber,' Brice said. He was just behind the door now.

'Yeah, but we got to fix the faucet, mister,' Willis said. 'That's a city regulation, we'll get a fine we don't fix it.'

'Well, come back later,' Brice said.

'I can't come back later. I go off at five.'

'Shit,' Brice said, and he unlocked the door and opened it wide.

'Police officer,' Willis said. 'Don't move.'

Brice seemed *about* to move, in fact, but he changed his mind the moment he saw the gun in Willis' fist.

'What is this?' he asked, which was a reasonable question.

The two detectives were inside the room now. Carella closed and locked the door behind him. There was a rumpled bed opposite the door, but no one was in it.

'Where's the woman—' Willis asked.

'In the john,' Brice said. 'What the hell *is* this, would you mind telling me?'

'Get her out here,' Carella said.

'Come on out!' Brice yelled.

'Who is it?' a woman asked from behind the closed bathroom door.

'It's the fuzz. Come on out here, okay?'

'Well, okay,' she said. The door opened. The woman was naked. Well, almost naked. She was wearing blue stockings rolled to the knees, and she was wearing red high-heeled shoes. She was perhaps twenty-seven or twenty-eight, a woman who may have been considered pretty once upon a time, when knights roamed the earth and chivalry was the order of the day. But chivalry was dead, and so was the girl's spirit, slain in a thousand shoddy hotel rooms by a succession of faceless men, slain too by the tread marks running up and down the inside of both arms. The girl looked exactly like both of the things she was – a junkie and a hooker. There was nothing exciting about her nakedness. The detectives had seen naked corpses with as much life.

'Anybody else here?' Carella asked.

'There's nobody else here,' Brice said. 'Just the two of us.'

'Hal?' Carella said, and Willis went to check out the bathroom.

'What's the beef?' Brice asked.

'Where were you all day yesterday?' Carella asked.

'Why?'

'Here it is straight,' Carella said. 'Something happened to a policeman's wife. The policeman is somebody you know. So where were you yesterday?'

'Who's the policeman? Never mind, don't tell me. The son of a bitch who killed my brother, am I right?'

'That's right.'

'What happened to his wife? I hope somebody—'

'Where were you yesterday, Al?'

'*Mister* Brice, if you don't mind. I done my time, I'm a private citizen now, you can call me *Mister* Brice.'

'Where were you yesterday, and cut the bullshit. We know you've a pair of weapons in this room, and unless you've got a permit for them ...'

'You find a gun in this room, I'll *eat* the fucking thing. Who told you I've got a gun in here?'

Willis came out of the bathroom, nodded to Carella, and then crossed the room to open the closet door.

'Let's start with three o'clock yesterday, okay?' Carella said.

'Let's start with *shit*,' Brice said. 'I was with Jenny all day yesterday. Whatever happened to Kling's wife—'

'You know his name, huh, Al?' Willis asked from the closet.

'I'll never forget that prick's name as long as I live,' Brice said.

'How about it, Jenny?'

'He was with me,' Jenny said.

'All day long?'

'All day.'

'You didn't happen to go to a wedding, did you?'

'No,' Jenny said.

'Where *did* you go?'

'We were up my apartment,' Jenny said.

'If you've got your own apartment, why'd you come here?'

''Cause I got a roommate, and she came home around eleven, and Al and me still wanted to be together.'

'What's your roommate's name?' Carella asked.

'Glenda.'

'Glenda what?'

'Glenda Manning.'

'Is that her real name?'

'It's real enough. It's what's on the mailbox.'

'Where?'

'1142 Jericho.'

'Is she there now?'

'I don't now where she is.'

'Is there a phone in the apartment?'

'Why?'

'Because I want to call her and ask her if you and Al were there last night when she came in at eleven.'

'Sure, go ahead,' Jenny said. 'The number's Halifax 4-3071.'

Carella went to the room phone and lifted the receiver. The desk clerk came on, and he told him what number he wanted. From the closet, Willis said, 'No guns in the room, huh, Al? What do you suppose these are?' He held up a holstered .38 and a .357 Magnum wrapped in flannel, its long barrel protruding from the folds of the cloth.

'I don't know, what are they?' Brice said.

'They're a pair of kosher pickles,' Willis said.

'I never seen them before in my life.'

'Never, huh?'

'Never,' Brice said. 'Must belong to the guy who checked out.'

'Mm-huh,' Willis said.

Into the phone, Carella said, 'Let me talk to Glenda Manning, please.'

'This is Glenda,' a woman's voice said.

'This is Detective Steve Carella,' he said. 'I want to ask you some questions.'

'Yes, Officer, what about?' Glenda said. 'If someone has made a complaint about this telephone number ...'

'This isn't the Vice Squad,' Carella said. 'Relax.'

'Why shouldn't I relax, anyway?' Glenda said. 'Even if it *is* the Vice Squad.'

'Glenda, where were you at eleven o'clock last night?' Carella asked.

'Why?'

'Routine investigation,' he said. 'Where were you?'

'Here.'

'Were you there all night?'

'No.'

'What time did you get there?'

'Just *about* eleven, in fact.'

'Can anybody verify that?'

'Sure.'

'Who?'

'My roommate and her boyfriend. They were here when I come in.'

'That was about eleven o'clock, you say?'

'That's right. We had a cup of coffee together, and then they left around a quarter to twelve.'

'Okay, Glenda.'

'Why, what happened?' Glenda asked.

'Nothing.'

'Then why do you want to know where I was at eleven o'clock last night?'

'Forget it,' Carella said. 'You've got nothing to worry about.' He put the phone back on the cradle.

'Okay, Al,' Willis said, 'where'd you get these pieces?'

'They're not mine. I already told you. Somebody must've left them in the room here.'

Willis sighed.

Carella looked at him.

'Worth the collar?' Willis asked.

'Any other time, yeah,' Carella said. 'Right now, we don't need the headache. So long, Brice, keep your nose clean. We get anything even *smelling* of those pieces, we'll be knocking on your door.'

Willis threw both guns onto the bed.

'Nice meeting you, miss,' he said.

'My pleasure,' she answered unconvincingly.

eight

By twenty minutes to midnight, Fat Ollie Weeks had almost reached the end of the trail. With the help of Kling, Cutler, and Pike, he had matched up photographs of husbands and wives, boyfriends and girl friends, boyfriends and boyfriends, and (in one instance) girl friend and girl friend. He had been left with pictures of four unidentified men and three unidentified women, and he had then gone over the invitation list in search of men and women who had been invited *alone* to the wedding and reception. There were eighteen such names on the list. Kling told him that all of the invited singles had been encouraged to bring a guest if they liked. So when Ollie left the hotel, he had a list of the eighteen in his pocket, together with photographs of the unidentified seven. By twenty minutes to midnight, he had checked out seventeen of the eighteen names, and had identified all but one person – a blond young man who'd appeared in several of the photographs taken at the church, but in none of the photographs taken at the reception. Ollie's task might have been a tedious one had it not been for two things: (1) he actually *liked* legwork, and (2) all of the women he spoke to that night were beautiful.

The last person on his list was a woman named Linda Hackett, and he knew *she* wasn't beautiful because she'd been pointed out to him in photographs taken at the wedding and the reception. 'Miss Linda Hackett', as she'd been referred to by both Cutler and Pike (as though they were somehow referring to royalty), was the editor of a fashion magazine, a formidable-looking broad in her early sixties, substantial of bosom (the way a pouter pigeon is), harsh of eye, fierce of visage, and (according to Cutler) probably cloven of hoof as well. Ollie was tired. All he wanted to do was go home, pour himself a drink, watch some television, and then go to sleep. But the possibility existed that Miss Linda Hackett had needed an escort for the festivities yesterday, and had asked the blond young man to serve in that capacity. Ollie rang the doorbell.

'Who is it?' a woman's voice asked.

'It's the police, miss,' Ollie said.

'The police?'

'Yes, miss.'

'Just a minute.'

He waited. He heard her unlocking the door, and then the door opened just a crack, restrained by a night chain. He held up his shield. 'Detective Oliver Weeks,' he said. 'I'd like to talk to Miss Linda Hackett, please.

'I am Miss Linda Hackett.'

'Miss Hackett,' he said, 'I would like to ask you a few questions, if you wouldn't mind taking off the chain and letting me in.'

'It's almost midnight,' she said. 'I was just getting ready for bed.'

'I shall try to be as brief as possible,' Ollie said, and cleared his throat.

'Well ...'

'Please, Miss Hackett, this is of extreme importance.'

'All right,' she said. 'But you'll have to wait a minute.'

'Certainly,' he said.

She closed the door. Ollie figured she was going to put on a bathrobe or something. He further figured that a woman, for some strange reason, sometimes took ten or twelve minutes to put on a bathrobe, whereas the same action usually took a man a minute and a half. Sighing, he pulled a cigarette from the package in his breast pocket, lit it, and had smoked it down almost to the filter tip when he heard the night chain being taken off the door. He ground out the butt, and looked at his watch. It was ten minutes to twelve. Miss Linda Hackett opened the door.

If anything, she seemed much more formidable in person that she had in her photographs. The photographs had given no real impression of height, but standing outside her door, Ollie realized she was at least five feet ten inches tall, if not taller, and rather wide of shoulder. Her face was rock-hard, her nose, mouth and massive jaw chiselled from Mount Rushmore. She possessed all the delicate femininity and grace of a roller-derby queen or a female wrestler – and yet she was the editor of one of the most influential fashion magazines in the world.

'Come in,' she said.

Sighing, Ollie followed her into the living room and took a seat beside her on the sofa. He took out his photographs, cleared his throat again, and by way of preamble said, 'I am going to show you some pictures taken at Augusta Blair's wedding yesterday, and I am going to ask you if you recognize the young man in these photographs.'

'Why?' Miss Linda Hackett asked.

'I can't tell you why,' Ollie said.

'You come here in the middle of the night—'

'Yes, but—'

'All right, let me see the pictures. You people really take the cake. Where the hell were you when my apartment was robbed last July?'

'Burglarized,' Ollie said.

'Yes, where the hell were you then?'

'This is not my precinct,' Ollie said. 'My precinct is the Eight-Three.'

'Then what are you doing here in the middle of the night with pictures for me to look at?'

'Well,' Ollie said, 'it's too complicated to explain.'

'I'll just *bet* it is,' she said. 'Let me see the damn pictures. I've got an eight o'clock meeting tomorrow morning, do you know that?'

'I'm sorry, I didn't realize that,' Ollie said.

'Let me see the damn pictures.'

He showed her the pictures.

'This is the man,' he said. 'This blond man. Do you know him?'

'This one?'

'Yes.'

'Who is he supposed to be?'

'Huh? What do you mean?' Ollie asked.

'Well, what's he *done*? Did he rob one of the guests or something?'

'I'm not at liberty to tell you anything about the case,' Ollie said. 'Do you recognize him?'

'Let me see those other pictures. Are they all of him?'

'Yes.'

'Let me see them. Where were these taken? At the church?'

'Yes.'

'Mm,' she said, and studied the pictures.

The man in question seemed to be in his late twenties, a thin-faced man with longish, straight blond hair and light eyes. In each of the pictures he was staring directly ahead of him, his mouth unsmiling.

'What's he *looking* at?'

'Well, those were taken inside the church,' Ollie said. 'He was probably watching the ceremony.'

'He looks very creepy,' she said, and suddenly looked up. 'Don't you think he looks creepy?'

'Yes, he does,' Ollie said.

'Jesus, he looks creepy,' she said, and shuddered.

'Do you recognize him?' Ollie said.

'No,' she said.

He was sitting just inside the door.

Augusta had heard him entering the room some ten minutes ago. He had not said anything in all that time, but she knew he was sitting there, watching her. When his voice came, it startled her.

'Your husband has blond hair,' he said.

She nodded. She could not answer him because he had replaced the gag the moment they'd concluded their earlier conversation, though he had not bothered to stuff anything into her mouth this time, had only wrapped the thick adhesive tape tightly across it and around the back of her head. That had been sometime after three-thirty; he had mentioned the time to her. She was ravenously hungry now, and knew she would accept food if he offered it to her. She made a sound deep in her throat to let him know she wished him to remove the gag again. He either did not hear her or pretended not to.

'What colour do you think my hair is?' he asked.

She shook her head. She knew what colour his hair was, of course; she had seen it when he'd burst hatless into the hotel room. His hair was blond. And his eyes above the surgical mask . . .

'You do not know?' he asked.

Again she shook her head.

'Ah, but you *saw* me,' he chided gently. 'At the hotel. *Surely* you noticed the colour of my hair.'

She made a sound behind the gag again.

'Something?' he asked.

She lifted her chin, twisted her head, tried to indicate to him that she wished the gag removed from her mouth. And in doing so, felt completely dependent upon him, and felt again a helpless rage.

'Ah, the adhesive,' he said. 'Do you wish the adhesive removed? Is that it?'

She nodded.

'You wish to talk to me?'

She nodded again.

'I will not talk to you if you continue to lie,' he said, and she heard him rising from the chair. A moment later she heard him closing and locking the door to the room.

He did not return for what seemed like a very long time.

'Augusta?' he whispered. 'Are you asleep?'

She shook her head.

'Do you know what time it is?'

She shook her head again.

'It's two o'clock in the morning. You should try to sleep, Augusta. Or would you prefer to talk?'

She nodded.

'But you must not lie to me again. You lied to me earlier. You said you didn't know what colour my hair is. You *do* know what colour it is, don't you?'

Wearily, she nodded.

'Shall I remove the adhesive? You must promise not to scream. Here,' he said, 'feel.' He had moved to her side, and she felt now the cold steel of the scalpel against her throat. 'You know what that is,' he said. 'I will use it if you scream. So,' he said, and slid the blade flat under the adhesive, and then twisted it, and cut the tape, and pulled it free.

'Thank you,' she said.

'You're quite welcome,' he said. 'Are you hungry?'

'Yes.'

'I thought you might be. You need not be afraid of me, Augusta.'

'I'm not afraid of you,' she lied.

'I shall prepare you something to eat in a moment.'

'Thank you.'

'What colour is my hair, Augusta? Please don't lie this time.'

'Blond,' she said.

'Yes. And my eyes?'

'Blue.'

'You had a very good look at me.'

'Yes.'

'Why did you lie? Were you worried that if you could identify me, I might harm you?'

'Why would you want to harm me?' she asked.

'Is that what you thought? That I might harm you?'

'Why am I here?' she asked.

'Augusta, please, you are making me angry again,' he said. 'When I ask you something, please answer it. I know you have many questions, but *my* questions come first, do you understand that?'

'Yes,' she said.

'*Why* do my questions come first?' he asked.

'Because ...' She shook her head. She did not know what answer he wanted from her.

'Because I am the one who has the scalpel,' he said.

'Yes,' she said.

'And you are the one who is helplessly bound.'

'Yes.'

'Do you realize *just* how helpless you are, Augusta?'

'Yes.'

'I *could* in fact harm you if I wished to.'

'But you said ...'

'Yes, what did I say?'

'That you wouldn't harm me.'

'No, I did not say that, Augusta.'

'I thought ...'

'You must listen more carefully.'

'I thought that was what you said.'

'No. If you weren't so intent on asking questions of your own, then perhaps you would listen more carefully.'

'Yes, I'll try to listen,' she said.

'You must.'

'Yes.'

'I did *not* say I wouldn't harm you. I asked if you *thought* I might harm you. Isn't that so?'

'Yes, I remember now.'

'And you did not answer my question. Would you like to answer it now? I'll repeat it for you. I asked if—'

'I remember what you asked.'

'Please don't interrupt, Augusta. You make me very impatient.'

'I'm sorry, I ...'

'Augusta, do you want me to put the adhesive on again?'

'No. No, I don't.'

'Then please speak only when I *ask* you to speak. All right?'

'Yes, all right.'

'I asked you why you lied to me. I asked whether you were worried that I might harm you if you could identify me.'

'Yes, I remember that.'

'Is that why you lied to me, Augusta?'

'Yes.'

'But surely I *had* to know you'd seen me.'

'Yes, but you were wearing a surgical mask. I still don't really know what you look like. The mask covered—'

'You're trying to protect yourself again, aren't you?' he said. 'By saying you still don't know what I look like?'

'I suppose so, yes. But it's true, you know. There *are* lots of people with blond hair and ...'

'But you *are* trying to protect yourself?'

'Yes. Yes, I am. Yes.'

'Because you still feel I might harm you.'

'Yes.'

'I might indeed,' he said, and laughed. He seized her chin then, and taped her mouth again, and swiftly left the room.

On the floor Augusta began trembling violently.

She heard the key turning in the lock, and then the door opened. He came to where she was lying near the wall, and stood there silently for what seemed like a very long time.

'Augusta,' he said at last. 'I do not wish to keep you gagged. Perhaps if I explain your situation, you will realize how foolish it would be to scream. We are in a three-storey brownstone, Augusta, on the top floor of the building. The first two floors are rented by a retired optometrist and his wife. They go to Florida at the beginning of November each year. We are quite alone in the building, Augusta. The room we are in was a very large pantry at one time. I have used it for storage ever since I moved into the apartment. It is quite empty now. I emptied it last month, after I decided what had to be done. Do you understand?'

She nodded.

'Fine,' he said, and cut the tape and pulled it free. She did not scream, but only because she was afraid of the scalpel. She did not believe for a moment that they were alone together in a three-storey brownstone; if indeed he did not gag her again, she would scream as soon as he left her alone in the room.

'I've made you some soup,' he said. 'You shall have to sit up. I shall have to untie your hands.'

'Good,' she said.

'You wish your hands untied?'

'Yes.'

'And your feet, too?'

'Yes.'

'No,' he said, and laughed. 'Your feet will stay as they are. I'm going to cut the adhesive that is holding your hands behind your back. Please don't try to strike out at me when your hands are free. Seriously, I will use the scalpel if I have to. I want your promise. Otherwise, I'll throw the soup in the toilet bowl and forget about feeding you.'

'I promise,' she said.

'And about screaming. Seriously, no one will hear you but me. I advise you not to scream. I become violent.'

He said the words so earnestly, so matter-of-factly that she believed him at once.

'I won't scream,' she said.

'It will be better,' he said, and cut the tape on her hands. She was tempted to reach up for the blindfold at once, pull the blindfold loose – but she remembered the scalpel again.

'Is that better?' he said.

'Yes, thank you.'

'Come,' he said, and pulled her to the wall, and propped her against it. She sat with her hands in her lap while he spoon-fed her. The soup was delicious. She did not know what kind of soup it was, but she tasted what she thought were meatballs in it, and noodles, and celery. She kept her hands folded in her lap, opening her mouth to accept the spoon each time it touched her lips. He made small sounds of satisfaction as she ate the soup, and when at last he said, 'All gone, Augusta,' it was rather like a father talking to a small child.

'Thank you,' she said. 'That was very good.'

'Am I taking good care of you, Augusta?'

'Yes, you are. The soup was very good,' she said.

'Thank you. I'm trying to take very good care of you.'

'You are. But ...'

'But you would like to be free.'

She hesitated. Then, very softly, she said, 'Yes.'

'Then I will free you,' he said.

'What?'

'Did you not hear me?'

'Yes, but ...'

'I will free you, Augusta.'

'You're joking,' she said. 'You're trying to torment me.'

'No, no, I will indeed free you.'

'Please, will you?' she said.

'Yes.'

'Thank you,' she said. 'Oh God, thank you. And when you let me go, I promise I won't—'

'Let you go?' he said.

'Yes, you—'

'No, I didn't say I would let you go.'

'You said—'

'I said I would *free* you. I meant I would untie your feet.'

'I thought—'

'You're interrupting again, Augusta.'

'I'm sorry, I—'

'Why did you marry him, Augusta?'

'I ... please, I ... please, let me go. I promise I won't tell anyone what you—'

'I'm going to untie your feet,' he said. 'The door has a deadbolt on it. From either side, it can be opened only with a key. Do not run for the door when I untie you.'

'No. No, I won't,' she said.

She heard the tape tearing, and suddenly her ankles were free.

'I'm going to take off the blindfold now,' he said. 'There are no windows in the room, there is only the door, that is all. It would be foolish for you to try to escape before the ceremony, Augusta, but—'

'What ceremony?' she asked at once.

'You constantly interrupt,' he said.

'I'm sorry. But what—'

'I don't think you will try to escape,' he said.

'That's right, I won't try to escape. But what cere—'

'Still, I must be gone part of the day, you know. I'm a working man, you know. And though the door will be locked, I could not risk your somehow opening it, and getting out of the room, and running down the street.'

'I wouldn't do that. Really,' she said, 'I—'

'Still, I must protect myself against that possibility,' he said, and laughed.

She smelled a familiar aroma, and started to back away from the sound of his voice, and collided with the wall, and was trying to rip the tape from her eyes when he pulled her hands away and clapped the chloroform-soaked rag over her nose and mouth again. She screamed. She screamed at the top of her lungs.

But no one came to help her.

nine

At eight o'clock on Tuesday morning, as Carella, Kling, and Fat Ollie Weeks were wading through record folders at the Identification Section downtown, Arthur Brown took a call in the squadron of the 87th.

'Detective Brown?' The Gaucho said.

'Yes, Palacios, what've you got?'

'Maybe something, maybe not.'

'Let me hear.'

'You know La Via de Putas?'

'I know it.'

'There's a place there called Mama Inez, eh?'

'Yes, I know the place.'

'Okay. Was last night a guy in there with one of the hookers, eh? And he drinks too much, he tells the girl he finally has his revenge now. She says, "*What* revenge now, what are you talking about, eh?" And he tells her, his revenge on a cop.'

'What cop?'

'He doesn't tell her this.'

'What's the guy's name?'

'He's a regular there, he goes every Monday night, he always asks for a black girl. He digs black girls, eh? It doesn't matter she's fat, she's skinny, she's bald. She just has to be black.'

'Black is beautiful,' Brown said dryly. 'What's his name?'

'His name is Anthony Hill. Mama Inez don't know where he lives, but she thinks it's up in Riverhead, eh? He's a married man, so like if you go knocking on his door, don't mention you found out about him from a lady who runs a whorehouse.'

'Yeah, thanks, Palacios.'

'Let me know if it turns out good, eh?'

'I'll let you know.'

Brown hung up, and walked to where Meyer Meyer was sitting at his desk leafing through Kling's arrest folders.

'Meyer, that was The Gaucho,' he said. 'Guy in Mama Inez's place last night, told one of the girl's he'd finally got his revenge on some cop. Think it's worth a try?'

'Right now,' Meyer said, '*anything*'s worth a try.'

The telephone directory listed an Anthony Phillip Hill at 1148 Lowery Drive in Riverhead. The detectives drove uptown and crosstown, and pulled up in front of the yellow brick apartment building at a little past nine o'clock. The row of mailboxes in the lobby informed them A. P. Hill was in apartment 44. They took the elevator up to the fourth floor and knocked on the door.

'Who is it?' a woman called.

'Police,' Brown said.

'Police?' she answered. 'You've got to be kidding.'

She opened the door and peered out into the corridor. She was a slatternly brunette in her late thirties, her hair in curlers, her dark eyes narrow with suspicion. She looked first at Brown and then at Meyer, and then said, 'You've got badges, I suppose.'

'We've got badges,' Brown said wearily, and flashed the tin. The woman studied the shield carefully, as though certain Brown was an impostor. When she was satisfied that she was indeed looking at a detective's shield, she turned to Meyer and said, 'Where's *yours*?'

'Why?' Meyer said. 'Isn't his good enough?'

'I don't let nobody in this apartment without identification,' the woman said.

Meyer sighed and took out a small leather case from his hip pocket. He opened this to his shield and his ID card, and as the woman studied them he said, 'We're looking for a man named Anthony Hill. Would he be home right now?'

'He would not be home right now,' the woman said.

'Okay to put this away?' Meyer asked.

'Yes, I guess you're a cop,' she said.

'Are you *Mrs* Hill?' Brown asked.

'Agnes Hill,' she said, and nodded.

'Know where we can find your husband?'

'He's at work. Why do you want him?'

'Mrs Hill, has your husband ever been in trouble with the law?'

'Never. What do you mean? Tony? Never. The law? Never. What do you mean? Trouble with the law?'

'Yes, ma'am.'

'Never.'

'Where does he work?'

'At the market on Meridian and Folger. He's the manager at the market there. What do you mean, trouble with the law? What kind of trouble with the law?'

'With a policeman,' Meyer said.

'A policeman?'

'A cop,' Brown said.

'Anthony Phillip Hill is a law-abiding citizen,' his wife said.

Anthony Phillip Hill was a man in his middle forties, with a round moon face, ruddy cheeks, blue eyes, bushy brown eyebrows, and a head not quite as bald as Meyer Meyer's, but getting there fast. He was wearing a long white apron, and he expressed no surprise when the detectives came into the supermarket. Both Brown and Meyer automatically assumed his wife had telephoned ahead to warn him they were on the way. Hill did not even faintly resemble the thin blond man in the photographs taken at the church, but the detectives could not dismiss him on this count alone. The possibility existed that the man in the photographs had been hired to abduct Augusta – a slim possibility, true, but they recognized it as such, and were merely trying to touch all bases in a game they were still losing. Anthony Hill had mentioned to a prostitute that he'd finally got his revenge on a cop. That's why they were there; Kling was a cop.

'I'll get right to it, Mr Hill,' Brown said. 'Last night you were with a hooker in a whorehouse on—'

'Excuse me,' Hill said, 'but last night I was here taking inventory.'

'No, last night you were—'

'I take inventory every Monday night,' Hill said.

'Sure,' Brown said. 'But *last* night you were in a house of prostitution run by a fat old broad named Mama Inez, and that's downtown on Mason Avenue, otherwise known as La Via de Putas, which translates into English as The Street of Whores. Now, that's where you were last night, Mr Hill, so let's stop waltzing around, okay, and get down to business.'

'You're making a mistake,' Hill said. 'I certainly hope you didn't tell any of this to my wife.'

'No, not *yet*, we haven't told any of this to your wife,' Meyer said, and there was such a note of ominous warning in his voice that Hill turned to him immediately. The two men looked at each other. 'That's right,' Meyer said, and nodded. 'So you want to talk to us, or what?'

'What do you want to talk about?'

'Who's this cop you got your revenge on?' Brown asked.

'What?'

'He a cop who arrested you one time?'

'You ever been in trouble with the law?' Meyer said.

'Of *course* not,' Hill said.

'We can check,' Meyer said.

'So check.'

'You've never been arrested, huh?'

'Never.'

'Then who's the cop you were talking about?'

'I don't know what you mean.'

'You were drunk last night, and you told this hooker you'd finally got your revenge on some cop. Now, who's the cop?'

'Oh,' Hill said.

'Yeah, *oh*. Who is he?'

'It's the cop here.'

'Where?'

'Here. On the beat here.'

'What's his name?'

'Cassidy. Patrolman Cassidy.'

'What about him?'

'It's a long story.'

'We've got plenty of time.'

It really *was* a long story. It was also a boring story. It was pointless, too, and a remarkable waste of time. They fidgeted while they listened to it. When Hill ended the story, there was a long pregnant silence. Then Brown said, 'Let me get this straight.'

'Yes, sir,' Hill said.

'This cop Cassidy is new on the beat.'

'Yes, sir. He's been here for two months now.'

'And he's begun giving you static about the boxes out back.'

'Yes, sir. The corrugated-cardboard cartons. The cartons the merchandise arrives in. We use some of them at the checkout for when people have bottles or—'

'Yeah, yeah,' Brown said.

'—other heavy items that might tear a bag.'

'Yeah. So what you *used* to do, if I understand this correctly—'

'That's right,' Hill said, and nodded.

'—what you *used* to do before Cassidy came on the beat, what you used to do was pile the cartons out back there every day, and your garbage man would come and pick them up on Mondays and Thursdays.'

'That's right,' Hill said, and nodded again. 'But Cassidy said it was a violation.'

'It *is* a violation,' Meyer said.

'That's what Cassidy said,' Hill said.

'He was right. It's a violation to have those boxes standing out there all the time unless it's the day the garbage man is coming to pick them up. That's a fire hazard, all those cartons standing out there.'

'Yes, that's what Cassidy said.'

'So what happened?'

'He wrote a ticket, and I had to go to court, and it cost me a fifty-dollar fine. I told the judge I'd been stacking my cartons out there since the beginning of time and nobody's said anything about it, and the judge said, "Well, it's a violation, and we can't fault the splendid work this police officer has done." That's what the judge said.'

'He was right,' Meyer said. 'It *is* a violation.'

'That's what the judge said, and also what Cassidy said,' Hill said.

'So now,' Brown said, 'if I understand this correctly ...'

'What I do now is I keep the cartons inside, except on the days the garbage man is coming. We've got this storeroom just to the right of the meat counter, if you'd like to see it ...'

'No, that's all right,' Brown said.

'It's where I keep the cartons now, except Mondays and Thursdays, when I put them outside for the garbage man.'

'That would be proper,' Meyer said. 'That wouldn't be a violation.'

'What I don't understand is how you got your revenge on Cassidy,' Brown said.

'Oh, that was a hot one,' Hill said, and chuckled, remembering it all over again.

'Would you mind explaining it again, please?'

'Not at all,' Hill said, still chuckling. 'I didn't put the cartons out.'

'I understand that. What you do is you put them out on Mondays and Thursdays when the—'

'No, no.'

'No?'

'No.'

'Then, what?' Brown said.

'I didn't put them out at *all*! I got the idea last month. What's today's date?'

'Tuesday, the eleventh,' Meyer said.

'Right. I got the idea on October twenty-fourth, the day after I paid the fifty-dollar fine. That was when I stopped putting out the cartons. Because Cassidy comes around to check, you know. He comes around to make sure there's nothing out back there except on Mondays and Thursdays, when the garbage man is coming. The twenty-fourth was a Thursday, and I stopped putting out the cartons on that day, even though the carbage man was coming. And I didn't put them out the following Monday, either. Nor the Thursday after that, nor the Monday after ...'

'I get the idea,' Brown said.

'Five whole *garbage* collections!' Hill said, and burst out laughing. 'Five whole collections, I didn't put the cartons out! And Cassidy snooping around out back there to make sure I wasn't doing anything wrong, but not a carton in sight for him to see. You know why?'

'Why?' Meyer asked.

'Because I had them all in the storeroom! I wouldn't put them out! I was hoarding those cardboard cartons as if they were made of solid gold.'

'Then what?' Brown said.

'Then yesterday was Monday. Garbage collection day, right?'

'Right.'

'I hauled out those cartons. I carried them out of the storeroom. I did it personally. Hundred of cartons. *Thousands* of of them! I piled them up out back. It looked like a fortress out back there. Cassidy walked by about ten o'clock in the morning, before the garbage truck got here. His teeth almost fell out of his mouth. I could see him trying to figure out whether it was a violation or not, but I knew it wasn't, I was doing everything according to the letter. Oh God,' Hill said, and began laughing again, 'you should have seen the look on Cassidy's face.'

'So that was your revenge,' Brown said.

'Yes, sir. That was my revenge.'

'But didn't all those boxes piled up in the storeroom cause a problem?'

'Oh sure,' Hill said. 'Could hardly get anything else *in* there. But it was worth it, believe me. Just seeing the look on Cassidy's face, it was worth all the inconvenience.'

'Revenge is sweet,' Brown said dryly.

'Yes, sir, it most certainly is,' Hill said, beaming.

Judging from the photographs taken inside the church, they were possibly (but only possibly) looking for a white Caucasian male, approximately five feet seven or eight inches tall, twenty-five to thirty years old, with light eyes, no visible scars, wearing a dark suit, a white shirt, a narrow dark tie, and a dark overcoat. None of the photos had been close-ups, but Alexander Pike had blown them up for the police, and the enlargements showed some wrinkles around the man's eyes and mouth, which had caused them to estimate his age slightly higher than a perusal of the smaller prints had at first led them to believe. The height was strictly surmise; the man was sitting in all of the photographs and an exact height was impossible to ascertain, but judging from the size of his head and trunk, the educated guess put him in the medium-height range. The overcoat was folded on his lap and visible in only two of the pictures, both of which had been shot from the side aisle, directly across the pew in which the blond man was sitting as Augusta came down the centre aisle.

The Identification Section was computerized, automated, and almost completely up to date, the lag between an actual arrest and the filing of a record being estimated (by the IS, admittedly biased) at seventy-two hours. The files were cross-indexed as well, so that if someone was looking for a burglar, say, with an MO of pissing in the icebox after he'd finished ransacking an apartment, and the burglar had a knife scar on his right cheek and a tattoo of a dancing girl who wiggled her breasts when a biceps was flexed – why, the buttons for BURGLARY and URINATION and TATTOOS would be pressed, and the system would deliver the name, description, arrest record, case dispositions, prison and parole records, and current status of anyone so gifted as to qualify in all those categories. All Carella, Kling, and Ollie *really* had to go on, though, was the description of the man who might or might not have abducted Augusta – the possibility existed that the man in the photographs was simply a passing stranger who loved to watch wedding ceremonies and had gone into the church to pass the time on a wintry day. They asked the IS attendant to punch out KIDNAPPING for them, and then the physical description of the man whose pictures they had, and that was all they could put into the computer. The system delivered a stack of folders and photographs. None of the photographs matched the ones already in their possession.

'Let's put the pictures on television,' Ollie said.

'No,' Kling said immediately.

'Why not?'

'Because we don't want to do anything that might endanger Augusta,' Carella said.

'We flash those pictures on the telly,' Ollie said, 'we'll have two hundred calls inside of ten minutes.'

'We'll also have a kidnapper who—'

'The answer is no,' Kling said. 'Forget it.'

'I'll tell you the truth,' Ollie said, 'this doesn't look like a kidnapping to me. It's been almost thirty-six hours already, and not a peep from anybody about a ransom. Now, that doesn't look like a kidnapping, not in all my years on the force. I had a kidnapping once, must've been three, four years ago, the guys waited eleven hours before they made contact, but that was a very long time, believe me. You get a kidnapping, they usually let you know right off what's expected. Kidnapping's a business like any other kind of crime, guys are in it for the money. All they want is their fifty, a hundred, two hundred Gs, whatever it is, and they want it fast. They'll kill the victim only if they think they can be identified. Otherwise, they'll turn the person loose in the country someplace, let him wander around bare-assed in the night till he finds a police station or somebody's house he can make a phone call from. That's been my experience with kidnapping, anyway. So here we got a lady snatched from a hotel room Sunday night around eleven-thirty, and here it is nine-thirty Tuesday morning, and not a peep. That ain't a kidnapping, not the way *I* see it. That is, I don't now *what* it is, but it ain't a kidnapping.'

'What are you saying, Ollie?' Carella asked.

'I'm saying if it ain't a kidnapping, then it's something with a kook. And where you got a kook, you got serious trouble. You got danger already, you don't *have* to worry about danger from putting a picture on television.'

'Bert?'

'Yeah, I hear him.'

'Look at it this way, kid,' Ollie said. 'We got nothing else to go on. We flash those pictures, somebody recognizes him, we close in before he knows what hit him.'

'And suppose *he*'s watching television?' Kling said.

'Yeah, so what?'

'So he sees a picture of himself, and he knows we're on to him, and he does just what you said a kidnapper does if he thinks he's been identified. He kills the victim.'

'But this is a *kook*,' Ollie said, 'and *not* a kidnapper. With kooks, there're no rules. He might see himself on television and throw himself out of the window.'

'Or throw my *wife* out of the window instead. Thanks, Ollie, the answer is no.'

'Look, I got respect for your feelings,' Ollie said, 'but—'

'I don't know *what* we're dealing with here,' Kling said. 'He may be a kook, like you say, but he may also be a kidnapper who's playing it cool. And in a kidnapping case, if *I*'ve read the goddamn instruction manual correctly—'

'Easy does it, kid,' Ollie said.

'—the victim's safety is of prime importance, everything else is secondary to the victim's safety. And that has nothing to do with Augusta's being my wife, that's only good sound police work; you don't do anything that might endanger the victim. Okay, Ollie, I'm telling you that putting those pictures on television may cause that guy to go off the deep end, *especially* if he's a kook. And I can't take a chance on him hurting Augusta for some stupid mistake we made.'

'*You*'re the one making the mistake,' Ollie said. 'Those pictures should be sent to every television station in the city, and they should be sent right away. We're sitting on the only thing we've got – pictures of the guy who maybe did it. What else have we got, can you tell me? Not a damn thing.'

'I'm still betting we'll hear from him,' Kling said.

'Don't hold your breath,' Ollie said.

ten

There were no windows in the room, just as he had promised.

The only source of illumination was a light bulb screwed into a ceiling fixture and operated from a switch just inside the door. The light was on now. The lock on the door was a key-operated deadbolt; it could not be unlocked from either side without a key. She walked to the door and examined the lock, and realized it had been installed only recently; there were jagged splinters of unpainted wood around the lock in the otherwise white-painted door. Against the wall opposite the door, a plastic bowl of water rested on the floor, and alongside that a bowl with what appeared to be some sort of hash in it. She went to the bowl, picked it up, sniffed at the contents, and then put the bowl down on the floor again. It was cold in the room, there was no visible source of heat. She shivered with a sudden chill and crossed her arms over her breasts, hugging herself. In the apartment outside, she heard footsteps approaching the door. She backed away from it.

'Augusta?' he called.

She did not answer. She debated lying on the floor again, pretending to be still unconscious so that she could make a run for the door when he unlocked it. But would he enter the room without the scalpel in his hand? She doubted it. She knew the sharpness of that blade, and she feared it. But she feared he might use it, anyway, whether she attempted escape or not. She waited. She was beginning to tremble again, and she knew it was not from the cold.

'May I come in, Augusta? I know you're conscious, I heard you moving about.'

His idiotic politeness infuriated her. She was his prisoner, he could do with her whatever he wished, and yet he asked permission to enter the room.

'You *know* you can come in, why do you bother asking?' she said.

'Ah,' he said, and she heard a key being inserted into the

94

lock. The door opened. He stepped into the room and closed and locked the door behind him. 'How are you?' he asked pleasantly. 'Are you all right?'

'Yes, I'm fine,' she said. She was studying his face more closely than she had in the hotel room. She was memorizing the straight blond hair, and the slight scar in the blond eyebrow over his left eye, and the white flecks in the blue eyes, and the bump on the bridge of his nose, where perhaps the nose had once been broken, and the small mole at the right-hand corner of his mouth. He was wearing dark-blue trousers and a pale-blue turtleneck shirt. There was a gold ring on his right hand, with a violet-coloured stone that might have been amethyst; it appeared to be either a college or a high school graduation ring. He wore a wristwatch on his left wrist. His feet were encased in white sweat socks and sneakers.

'I have a surprise for you,' he said, and smiled. He turned abruptly then, and left the room without explanation, locking the door behind him. She moved into a corner of the room the moment he was gone, as though her position was more protected there in the right angle of two joining walls. In a little while she heard the key turning in the lock again. She watched the knob apprehensively. It turned, the door opened. He came into the room carrying a half-dozen or more garments on wire hangers. Holding these in his left hand, he extricated the key from the outside of the lock, and then closed the door and locked it from the inside. The clothing looked familiar. He saw her studying the garments, and smiled.

'Do you recognize them?' he asked.

'I'm ... not sure.'

'These were some of my favourites,' he said. 'I want you to put them on for me.'

'What are they?' she asked.

'You'll remember.'

'I've worn them before, haven't I?' she said.

'Yes. Yes, you have.'

'I've modelled them.'

'Yes, that's it exactly.'

She recognized most of the clothing now – the chambrayblue safari jacket and matching shorts she had modelled for *Mademoiselle*, the ruffled-edged cotton T-shirt and matching wrap-around skirt she had posed in for *Vogue*, yes, and wasn't that the high-yoked chemise she had worn for *Harper's Bazaar*? And there, the robe that—

'Would you hold these, please?' he asked. 'The floor is clean, I scrubbed it before you came, but I would rather not put them down.' He shrugged apologetically and extended the clothes to her. 'It will only be for a moment,' he said.

She held out her arms and he draped the garments across them, and turned and went to the door. She watched as he unlocked it again. He left the key in the keyway this time, and he left the door open behind him. But he did not go very far from the room. Just outside the door, Augusta could see a standing clothes rack and a straight-backed wooden chair. He carried the clothes rack into the room first, taking it to the far corner where Augusta had earlier retreated. Then he carried the chair in, and closed and locked the door, and set the chair down just inside it, and was preparing to sit when he said abruptly, 'Oh, I almost forgot.' He moved the chair away from the door again, and again inserted his key into the lock. 'Would you hang the clothes on the rack, please?' he said. 'I won't be a moment.' He unlocked the door, opened it, and went out. She heard him locking the door again from the other side.

The clothes rack was painted white, a simple standing rack with one vertical post to which were attached, at slanting angles and at varying heights, a series of pegs. She carried the clothes to the rack and hung them on the pegs. She noticed as she did so that at least one of the garments – the safari jacket – was in her size, and she quickly checked the others and learned that *all* of them were exactly her size. She wondered how he had known the size, and guessed he had got it from the suit she'd been wearing – but had he bought all this clothing *after* he'd taken her from the hotel room? One of the garments on the rack was a robe she had modelled for *Town & Country*.

She took it down, and was putting it on when the door opened again.

'What are you doing?' he said. He spoke the words very softly. 'Take that off.'

'I was a little chilly, I thought—'

'Take it off!' he said, his voice rising. 'Take it off this instant!'

Silently, she took off the robe, put it back on the hanger, and hung it on the rack. He was standing just inside the open door now. In his left hand he was holding a paper bag with the logo of one of the city's most expensive department stores on it.

'I did not give you permission,' he said.

'I didn't know I needed permission,' Augusta said. 'I was cold. It's cold in here.'

'You will do only what I tell you to do, when I tell you to do it. Is that clear?'

She did not answer.

'Is it?'

'Yes, yes,' she said.

'I don't believe I like that note of impatience in your voice, Augusta.'

'I'm sorry.'

He locked the door behind him, put the key into his pocket, moved the chair so that its back was against the door again, and then said, 'We are to have a fashion show.' He smiled and extended the small parcel he was holding. 'Here,' he said. 'Take it.'

She walked to where he was sitting, and took the paper bag from his hands. Inside the bag, she found a pair of pale-blue bikini panties and a blue bra. The panties were a size 5, the bra was a 34B.

'How did you know my sizes?' she asked.

'They were in *Vogue*,' he said. 'The April issue. Last year, don't you remember? "All about Augusta". Don't you remember?'

'Yes.'

'That was a very good article, Augusta.'

'Yes, it was.'

'It didn't mention Detective Bert Kling, though.'

'Well . . .'

'In an article titled "All About Augusta", it would hardly seem honest to neglect mentioning—'

'I guess the agency felt—'

'You're interrupting, Augusta.'

'I'm sorry.'

'That is truly a vile habit. In my home, if I ever interrupted, I was severely thrashed.'

'I won't interrupt again. I was only trying to explain why the article didn't mention Bert.'

'Ah, is that what you call him? Bert?'

'Yes.'

'And what does he call you?'

'Augusta. Or sometimes Gus. Or Gussie.'

'I prefer Augusta.'

'Actually, I do too.'

'Good. We are at least in agreement on something. Blue is your favourite colour, the article said. Is that true?'

'Yes.'

'Does the blue please you?'

'Yes, it's fine. When did you buy these clothes?'

'Last month,' he said. 'When I knew what had to be done.'

'You still haven't told me—'

'The ceremony will take place tomorrow evening,' he said.

'What ceremony?'

'You will see,' he said. 'My mother was a model, you know. In Europe, of course. But she was quite well-known.'

'What was her name?' Augusta said.

'You would not know it,' he said. 'This was long before your time. She was murdered,' he said. 'Yes. I was a small boy at the time. Someone broke into the house, a burglar, a rapist, who knows? I awakened to the sounds of my mother screaming.'

Augusta watched him. He seemed unaware of her presence now, seemed to be talking only to himself. His eyes were somewhat out of focus, as though he were drifting off to another place, a place he knew only too well – and dreaded.

'My father was a leather-goods salesman, he was away from home. I leaped out of bed, she was screaming, screaming. I ran across the parlour toward her bedroom – and the screaming stopped.' He nodded. 'Yes.' He nodded again. 'Yes,' he said, and fell silent for several moments, and then said, 'She was on the floor in a pool of her own blood. He had slit her throat.' He closed his eyes abruptly, squeezed them shut, and then opened them almost immediately. 'Well, that was a long time ago,' he said. 'I was just a small boy.'

'It must have been horrible for you.'

'Yes,' he said, and then shrugged, seemingly dismissing the entire matter. 'I think the pants suit will suit you nicely,' he said, and grinned. 'Do you understand the pun, Augusta?'

'What? I ...'

'The suit. The suit. The suit will suit you,' he said, and laughed. 'That's good, don't you think? The hardest thing to do in a second language is to make a pun.'

'What's your *first* language?' she asked.

'I come from Austria,' he said.

'Where in Austria?'

'Vienna. Do you know Austria?'

'I've skied there.'

'Yes, of course, how stupid of me! In the article—'

'Yes.'

'—it said you skied in Zürs one time. Yes, I remember now.' 'Do you ski?'

'No. No, I have never skied. Augusta,' he said, 'I wish you to take off the clothes you are now wearing and put on first the panties and brassiere, and then the suit.'

'If you'll leave the room ...'

'No,' he said, 'I'll stay here while you change. It will be more *intime, n'est-ce pas?* Do you speak French?'

'A little. I'll put on the clothes only if you—'

'No, no,' he said, and laughed. 'Really, Augusta, you are being quite ridiculous. I could have done to you whatever I wished while you were unconscious. You'll be pleased to learn I took no liberties. So now, when you—'

'I would like to go to the toilet,' she said.

'What?'

'I have to move my bowels,' she said.

A look of total revulsion crossed his face. He kept staring at her in utter disbelief, and then he rose abruptly and shoved the chair aside, and unlocked the door and went out of the room. She heard the lock clicking shut again, and rather suspected the fashion show had suddenly been cancelled. Smiling, she went to the wall opposite the door, and sat on the floor with her back against it. She felt a bit warmer now.

There was no time in the room.

He was her clock, she realized.

She dozed and awakened again. She sipped water from the bowl. She nibbled at the meat in the other bowl. When she grew cold again, she put on the long white robe over her clothes, and sat huddled on the floor, hugging herself. She dozed again.

When he came into the room again, he left the door open. He was wearing a dark-brown overcoat, and in the open V of the coat, she could see the collar of a white shirt, and a dark tie with a narrow knot. Behind him, from a window somewhere in the apartment, there was the faint wintry light of early morning.

'I must go to work now,' he said. His tone was colder than it had been.

'What time is it?' she asked.

'It's six-thirty a.m.'

'You go to work early,' she said.

'Yes,' he said.

'What sort of work do you do?'

'That is no concern of yours,' he said. 'I will return by three-thirty at the latest. I will prepare you for the ceremony then.'

'What sort of ceremony is it to be?' she asked.

'I see no harm in telling you,' he said.

'Yes, I'd really like to know.'

'We are to be married, Augusta,' he said.

'I'm already married.'

'Your marriage has not taken effect.'

'What do you mean?'

'It has not been consummated.'

She said nothing.

'Do you remember the wedding gown you wore in *Brides* magazine?'

'Yes.'

'I have it. I bought it for you.'

'Look I ... I appreciate what—'

'No, I don't think so,' he said.

'What?'

'I don't think you *do* appreciate the trouble I've gone to.'

'I do, really I do. But ...'

'I didn't know your shoe size, that's why I didn't buy any shoes. The article about you didn't mention your shoe size.'

'Probably because I have such big feet,' she said, and smiled.

'You shall have to be married barefooted,' he said.

'But, you see,' she said, refusing to enter into his delusion, 'I'm *already* married. I got married on Sunday afternoon. I'm Mrs Bertram ...'

'I was there at the church, you don't have to tell me.'

'Then you know I'm married.'

'Are you angry about the shoes?'

'You have a trick,' she said.

'Oh? What trick is that?'

'Of refusing to face reality.'

'There is only one reality,' he said. 'You are here, and you are mine. That is reality.'

'I'm *here*, that's reality, yes. But I'm not yours.'

'I'll be late for work,' he said, and looked at his watch.

'There's your trick again. I'm *mine*,' she said. 'I belong to *me*.'

'You *were* yours. You are no longer yours. You are mine. This afternoon, after the ceremony, I will demonstrate that to you.'

'Let's talk about reality again, okay?'

'Augusta, that *is* the reality. I will be home at three-thirty. I will take you to the bathroom, where you will bathe yourself

and anoint yourself with the perfume I've purchased –
L'Oriel *is* your favourite, am I correct? That's what the
article said. And then you will put on the white undergarments
I bought, and the blue garter, and the gown you modelled in
Brides. And then we shall have a simple wedding ceremony,
uniting us in the eyes of God.'

'No,' she said, 'I'm already—'

'Yes,' he insisted. 'And then we shall make love, Augusta.
I have been waiting a long time to make love to you. I have
been waiting since I first saw your photograph in a magazine.
That was more than two years ago, Augusta, you should not
have *dared* give yourself to another man. Two long years,
Augusta! I've loved you all that time, I've been waiting all
that time to possess you, yes, Augusta. When I saw you on
television doing a hair commercial – do you remember the
Clairol commercial? – saw you *moving*, Augusta, saw your
photographs suddenly coming to *life*, your hair floating on
the wind as you ran, how beautiful you looked, Augusta – I
waited for the commercial again. I sat before the set, waiting
for you to appear again, and finally I was rewarded – but ah,
how brief the commercial was, how long *are* those commercials? Thirty seconds? Sixty seconds?'

'They vary,' she answered automatically, and was suddenly
aware of the lunatic nightmare proportions of the conversation. She was discussing the length of television commercials
with a man who planned to marry her today in a fantasy
ceremony . . .

'I abuse myself with your photographs,' he said suddenly.
'Does that excite you? The thought of my doing such things
with your pictures?'

She did not answer him.

'But this afternoon I will actually possess you. We will be
married, Augusta, and then we will make love together.'

'No, we—'

'Yes,' he said. 'And then I will slit your throat.'

eleven

Steve Carella was at home shaving that Wednesday morning when the telephone rang. He put down his razor, went out into the bedroom, and picked up the telephone.

'Hello?' he said.

'Steve, Danny. You got a minute?'

'Sure, go ahead.'

'I'm sorry I'm calling you at home ...'

'That's okay, what've you got, Danny?'

'I located this guy Baal you're looking for. Manfred Baal, with a double *a*. I found out where he is.'

'Where?'

'Or at least I found out where he *works*. I don't know where he lives.'

'Where does he work?'

'Kane Construction Company, 307 South Beasley. He's working as a common labourer, I think this is just to tide him over till he can pull a stickup. He bought a gun, Steve, that's how I got a line on him.'

'What kind of gun?'

'A Smith & Wesson automatic. Bought it from a guy deals in stolen pieces. That's the route I was following, Steve. I figured a guy done time for robbery, first thing he's gonna do when he gets outside is plan another stickup. Okay. For a stickup, you need a piece. And there ain't no guy who's been in the joint who's gonna go buy his gun from a sporting-goods store. So I been asking around guys who deal in such things. And I hit pay dirt three o'clock this morning. I called the squadroom right away, and they told me you wouldn't be in till around a quarter to eight. I know it's earlier than that now, but I figured you might want to move on this fast, maybe be waiting for the guy when he gets to work. These construction companies start early.'

'Good, Danny.'

'This guy Baal is a foreigner, did you know that? He talks

with a foreign accent. That's what the guy who sold him the piece said.'

'Yeah, I've got his folder up at the squadroom,' Carella said.

'Well, good luck with it,' Danny said. 'I don't suppose he'll have the rod with him on the job, but you might be careful, anyway.'

'I always am,' Carella said.

'Okay, Steve, let me know.'

'I'll drop a little something in the mail.'

'No rush,' Danny said, and hung up.

Manfred Baal's folder identified him as a man who'd come to this country from his native Switzerland some thirty years ago. He was forty-seven years old, and had spent most of his years in the United States in prison. His hair was blond and his eyes were blue, but he did not otherwise resemble the man whose pictures Alexander Pike had taken in church. Fat Ollie and Carella went to talk to him only because they still had nothing else to go on, and were loath to eliminate the possibility that Augusta's abductor was only a hired hand performing a service for someone with a grievance. Baal had a grievance; Kling had sent him to prison for ten years. Baal had made his grievance known; he had in fact shouted it out in court on the day the judge sentenced him. He had pointed his finger at Kling and yelled across the length of the courtroom, 'You! I'm going to kill you one day, you hear? *You!*' The peace officers in the courtroom had dragged him out screaming and kicking, an auspicious beginning for his ten-year stretch at Castleview. Baal had been out of jail for close to a month now, and he still hadn't killed Kling; perhaps he'd mellowed behind the walls. But Augusta had been kidnapped on Sunday night, and Baal's threat echoed loud and clear on this Wednesday morning as they drove to the construction site. They had earlier called Kane Construction and spoken to a man named Di Giorgio who told them Baal was working on an apartment building at Weber and Tenth – they'd see the big sign as they drove up, a big red sign with the words Kane Construction on it in yellow. They had no trouble finding the sign *or* the construction site. Finding Baal was another thing again.

'Didn't show up today,' the foreman said.

'What?' Carella asked. There were jackhammers and pile drivers going everywhere around them, trucks grinding into gear, bulldozers shoving earth, sledges pounding against rock, pneumatic drills stuttering.

'I said he didn't show up today!' the foreman shouted.

'Did he call in sick or anything?'

'Nope.'

'Would you have his home address?'

'Me? No, I wouldn't have his home address. You can call the office, though, they probably got it on file there. What'd this guy do, anyway?'

'Where's the phone?' Carella said.

'In the shack there. What'd Baal do?'

Carella dialled Kane Construction, and talked to Di Giorgio again. Di Giorgio said Baal hadn't called there, either, but he said that wasn't too unusual with some of the unskilled labourers; they went out on the town the night before and just didn't bother showing up for work the next day. The address Baal had given the company when he was hired was for a rooming house on Oliver and Sixty-third. Carella jotted it down, thanked him, and then thanked the foreman, too, who asked again, 'What'd Baal do?'

'If we're lucky,' Ollie said, 'he at least done something.'

'Huh?' the foreman said.

She was alone in the apartment.

The entire place was still.

She had listened very carefully after he'd gone out of the room and locked the door. She had gone to the door instantly, and put her ear against it, listening the way Bert had told her *he* listened before entering a suspect premises. She had heard the front door of the apartment closing behind him, and then she had continued listening, her ear pressed to the wooden door, listening for footsteps approaching the storage room again, suspecting a trick. She did not have a watch, he had taken that from her, but she counted to sixty and then to sixty again, and again, and over again until she estimated that she'd been standing inside the door with her ear pressed to the wood for about fifteen minutes. In all that time, she had heard nothing. She had to assume he was really and truly gone.

He had left the clothing behind.

More important than that, he had left the wire hangers and the wooden clothes rack. He was a very careful man, he had installed a double keyway deadbolt on the door as soon as he'd decided to abduct her, a most methodical, most fastidious, foresighted person. But he had forgotten that he was dealing with a cop's wife, and he had neglected to notice that the door opened *into* the room, and that the hinge pins were on Augusta's side of the door. Quickly, she removed all the clothing from the rack and tossed it into one corner of the room. Then she dragged the rack over to the door, and opened up one of the wirehangers by twisting the curved hook away from the body.

She was ready to go to work.

The rooming house on Oliver and Sixty-third was a red brick building covered with the soot and grime of at least a century, four storeys, high, with a five-tiered stoop rising from the pavement to a wide concrete landing just before the entrance door. A man bundled in a heavy black overcoat and muffler, his hands in the pockets of his coat, was standing just to the right of the glass-panelled entrance door, staring out at the street. He seemed not to be watching Ollie and Carella as they climbed the steps, his focus concentrated instead on the kerb, where nothing was happening. But as Carella reached for the knob, he said abruptly, 'Who you looking for?'

'Manfred Baal,' Carella said.

'No Manfred Baal here,' the man said.

'Who're you?'

'Superintendent of the building. Ain't no Manfred Baal here.'

'He's a tall blond man with blue eyes,' Carella said. 'About forty-eight years old.'

'A greenhorn,' Ollie said. 'From Sweden or someplace.'

'Switzerland,' Carella said.

'Same difference,' Ollie said, and shrugged.

'That's Manfred Baal, all right,' the super said, 'but he don't live here no more.'

'Where *does* he live, would you know?'

'Nope.'

'When did he move out?'

'About a week, ten days ago.'

'And he didn't leave a forwarding address, huh?'

'Not with me he didn't. He might've told the post office where he was going, but I don't guess he done that, either. All the time he was living here, he never got a single piece of mail.'

'Have you rented the room he was living in?'

'Not yet, I haven't.

'Mind if we take a look at it?' Carella asked.

'What for?'

'What's your name, mister?' Ollie asked suddenly.

'Jonah Hobbs,' the super said.

'Jonah,' Ollie said, 'what room was Manny Baal living in?'

'Room twenty-four.'

'Jonah,' Ollie said, 'have you got a key for room twenty-four?'

'Of course I do.'

'Jonah,' Ollie said, 'you want to come upstairs with us and open the door to room twenty-four?'

'What for?' Hobbs said.

'Because if you don't open it for us, we're gonna kick the fuckin thing in,' Ollie said.

'I guess I'll open it for you,' Hobbs said.

He took them into the building and up to the second floor, where he unlocked a door at the end of the hall. The room was sparsely furnished, a single bed to the left of a window, a night table beside the bed, a lamp, a chair, a dresser with a mirror over it. The window was covered with a shade, which was drawn now. The bed was unmade. The room was spotlessly clean. Carella went to the window and raised the shade.

The brick wall of the adjacent building was some fifteen feet away across the shaftway. An old woman with a shawl over her shoulders was sitting at a window in the other building. As Carella raised the shade she turned her head sharply toward him and stared at him suspiciously.

'This room been cleaned since Baal moved out?' Ollie asked.

'Don't it look it?' Hobbs said.

'It looks it.' Ollie said. 'Was it?'

'It was.'

'Mm,' Ollie said, and went directly into the bathroom. Carella opened a closet door. There were eight wire hangers on the clothes bar. That was it. He closed the door. In the bathroom, Ollie was looking through the medicine cabinet.

'Anything?' Carella said.

'Dry as a bone,' Ollie answered, and came out into the room again. 'Who cleaned this joint?' he asked Hobbs.

'We've got a cleaning woman comes in,' Hobbs said.

'She here today?'

'She's here every day.'

'Where is she now?'

'What time is it?'

Ollie looked at his watch. 'Ten after nine,' he said.

'Then she's probably still up on the fourth floor.'

'I want to talk to her,' Ollie said.

Together, he and Carella followed Hobbs to the fourth floor. The cleaning woman was a black woman named Esther Johnson. It was clear from the beginning of their conversation that all she wanted to do was to get her work done without interruptions; the whereabouts of Manfred Baal was of no interest whatever to her. Impatiently, she tried to tell the detectives that she didn't know nothing about no Manfred Baal except she cleaned his room every day. Patiently, Ollie told her that he was precisely interested in the last time she had cleaned it, and in what she might have—

'I cleaned it last Tuesday,' Esther said.

'Had he moved out already?'

'Room was empty, I'd say the man had moved out.'

'Anything in the dresser?'

'Just the usual junk a man leaves behind when he's moving.'

'Like what?' Ollie said immediately. 'That's the kind of junk I'm interested in, Mrs Johnson. Matchbooks or—'

'It's *Miss* Johnson,' Esther said.

'*Miss* Johnson, forgive me, m'dear,' Ollie said in his W. C. Fields voice. Then, switching immediately to his natural voice, he said, 'Or an old address book, or maybe an appointment calendar.'

'Wasn't nothing like that in any of the drawers.'

'But there *was* junk in the drawers ...'

'That's right. A ball-point pen, as I recall, and a few pennies back there in the corner of the top drawer, and some paper clips. Like that.'

'How about the bathroom? Anything in the medicine cabinet there?'

'The cabinet was empty. I remember all I had to do was give the shelves a good wipe.'

'Anything in that basket under the sink?'

'Just some razor blades, stuff like that.'

'Stuff like what?'

'Like used razor blades. Like I told you.'

'And what else?'

'Some tissues. And a newspaper. That's all I can remember.'

'How about the closet?'

Esther looked at Hobbs. 'Shall I tell them about the whiskey?' she asked.

'What about the whiskey?' Ollie said at once.

'Had a dozen bottles of whiskey in there,' Esther said. 'Is it all right to tell them about the whiskey?'

'I don't see nothing wrong with telling them about the whiskey,' Hobbs said.

'What kind of whiskey?'

'All kinds,' Esther said. 'Scotch, gin, vodka, bourbon, all kinds of whiskey. Must've been at least a dozen bottles in there, ain't that right, Mr Hobbs?'

'Four*teen* bottles, to be exact,' Hobbs said. 'All of them sealed.'

'Man must've been a teetotaller,' Esther said. 'Never did

find a glass smelling of alcohol around here. And never did see an empty whiskey bottle in the trash container.'

'Fourteen bottles of unopened whiskey,' Ollie said. 'He left that whiskey here, huh?'

'Left it behind him,' Hobbs said.

'Think he forgot it?'

'Don't see how he could've forgot it,' Esther said. 'It was sittin right there on the closet floor.'

'Left behind fourteen bottles of whiskey,' Ollie said, and looked at Carella. 'Man doesn't drink, but he buys himself fourteen bottles of whiskey, and then leaves them behind when he moves out.'

'Maybe he was planning a party,' Hobbs said.

'Then why'd he leave the booze behind?'

'Maybe he changed his mind,' Hobbs said, and shrugged.

'Where's that whiskey now?' Ollie asked.

Hobbs and Esther looked at each other.

'Come on, come on,' Ollie said impatiently.

'Esther and me split it between us,' Hobbs said. 'I took the Scotch and the blended whiskey and a bottle of cognac and—'

'Yeah, I don't need an inventory,' Ollie said. 'Where's the whiskey now? Is any of it left?'

'Man only moved last Tuesday,' Hobbs said indignantly. 'I want you to know I'm just a social drinker, there's no way possible I could've drunk—'

'Where is it?' Ollie said. 'I want to see those bottles.'

The hinge pins had been painted into the hinges.

Augusta had broken off one of the pegs on the clothes rack, and tried using that as a makeshift mallet, hoping to chip away the paint. But the peg wasn't heavy enough, and however hard she struck at the hinge, the paint remained solidly caked to it. She had no idea what time it was, but she'd been working on just that single hinge for what seemed like hours. She had made no headway, and there were three hinges on the door, and he had told her he would be back in the apartment by three-thirty. She picked up the clothes rack now, picked it up in both hands, and using it like a battering ram, she began smashing at the middle hinge on the door.

A chip of paint flaked off.

There are liquor stores that stick their own store labels someplace on the bottles of whiskey or wine they sell. The particular bottles in Jonah Hobbs's possession carried stickers for Mercer's Wine & Liquor on Fortieth and The Stem. Fortieth Street was more than a mile from the rooming house on Sixty-third – the city rule of thumb being that twenty blocks equalled one linear mile. For some mysterious reason, the city's liquor stores seemed to proliferate more wildly than its bookstores, and there were perhaps half a dozen such booze emporiums within a four-block radius of the rooming house. Considering the proximity of so many juice joints, it seemed passing strange to Ollie and Carella that Baal would have travelled so far for his supply, especially when he didn't plan to *drink* any of it. They both had a few ideas on the subject even before they went to Mercer's Wine & Liquor. The store was owned and operated by a man named Lewis Mercer. They showed him the mug shot of Manfred Baal and asked if he'd ever been in the store.

'Oh yeah. Guy's a steady customer,' Mercer said.

'How long has he been coming here?'

'Only the past few weeks,' Mercer said. 'But he buys a lot.'

'How much does he buy?'

'At least a fifth every other day. Sometimes more. Like once he came in and bought a fifth of gin, and an orange liqueur. Guy must drink a lot. Well, I've seen heavier drinkers, that's true. Guys who'll knock off two quarts of the stuff each and every day. But those are your real rummies, they're already seeing things coming out of the walls, you know what I mean? This guy just likes his booze, that's all. Comes in, passes the time of day, walks around the shop making his choice – different kind of booze all the time.'

'What time did you say he comes in?'

'Same time every day. Twelve, twelve-thirty, something like that.'

Ollie looked up at the clock. 'Mr Mercer,' he said, 'we think you're being set up for a robbery.'

'What?' Mercer said.

'This man Baal has spent time in prison for armed robbery.'

'Yeah?' Mercer said, and shrugged. 'He seems like a very nice person.'

'There are very nice persons in prison,' Ollie said philosophically, 'who have murdered their wives and children. Mr Mercer, was Mr Baal in this store yesterday?'

'No, he wasn't,' Mercer said.

'Was he here on Monday?'

'Yes.'

'You said he comes in every other day. That means he'll be here today.'

'That's right.'

'Mr Mercer, we would like to wait for him. Is there a back room we can use?'

Manfred Baal did not come into the liquor store till one o'clock that afternoon. He walked directly to the counter behind which Lewis Mercer was standing, and was opening his mouth to say something when Ollie and Carella burst out of the back room. 'Police officers,' Ollie said, and noticed at once that the two centre buttons on Baal's overcoat were unbuttoned. Baal's hand moved into the opening and emerged an instant later holding a Smith & Wesson automatic. But by that time Ollie and Carella had both drawn their service revolvers, and Baal found himself staring into the muzzles of a pair of .38 Detective's Specials. He undoubtedly decided that he was on the losing end of the arms race, and immediately threw his gun onto the floor.

'I came here to buy a bottle of whiskey,' he said in mildly accented English. 'Ask the gentleman. I come in here every other day to buy whiskey.'

'We already asked the gentleman,' Ollie said.

'He will tell you,' Baal said.

'He already told us.'

'And I have a permit for the pistol,' Baal said.

'Let's see it,' Carella said.

'I do not have it with me.'

'Is it carry or premises?' Ollie asked.

'It is a carry permit.'

'The law says you've got to have the permit on your person at all times. If you haven't got it with you, that's tough shit, you're stuck with a gun violation.'

'Even so, you cannot charge me with armed robbery. I did not say anything to the gentleman. I was here to buy whiskey, and that is all.'

'Fine, we'll talk about it in the squadroom,' Carella said.

'The gun violation is all,' Baal said.

'Fine,' Carella said.

They talked to him for close to two hours.

They lied outrageously and so did he.

'We've had that joint staked out for close to a month now,' Ollie said. 'When we saw you starting to come in regular, we knew you were setting up a hit.'

'I was merely buying whiskey,' Baal said.

'Sure. Were you merely buying whiskey today?'

'Yes.'

'Then why'd you have that piece in your belt?'

'This is a dangerous city. That is why I have a permit to carry a pistol.'

'Manny, you are full of shit,' Ollie said. 'You're a man who's served time for armed robbery, you couldn't get a pistol permit if you stood on your head.'

'Oh, you know about that,' Baal said.

'Are you a dimwit or something?' Ollie asked. 'Don't you know what precinct this is? Don't you recognize this room? What the hell's the matter with you, Manny? This is the Eight-Seven, this is where Detective Kling works. You know that name, Manny?'

'No, I don't believe I do,' Baal said.

'He's the man you threatened to kill ten years ago.'

'I never threatened to kill anyone in my life,' Baal said.

'You made the threat in a courtroom in front of a hundred goddamn witnesses,' Ollie said.

'If I made such a threat, it was an idle one,' Baal said.

'Where were you Sunday night?' Carella asked.

'Why do you want to know?'

'It's important to us.'

'I do not have to talk to you at *all*,' Baal said. 'I know my rights.'

'You *ought* to know your fùckin rights, you moron,' Ollie said. 'We spent a half-hour explaining them to you.'

'I *do* know my rights.'

'And you said you'd talk to us without a lawyer here. Is that what you said, or isn't it?'

'That's when I thought we would be talking about the gun violation. If you want to talk about armed robbery, or about something that happened to this Detective Kling—'

'What do you know about that?' Carella said. 'About something happening to Kling?'

'If something has happened to him, I know nothing about it.'

'How about his wife?'

'What?'

'Something happening to his wife?' Ollie said.

'I will only talk about the gun violation,' Baal said. 'That's all you can charge me with. If you're trying to hang anything else on me—'

'What else *is* there to hang on you?' Carella said.

'Armed robbery. Or attempted robbery. Whatever. I did not hold up that store, and I did not *attempt* to hold up that store.'

'Did you do anything to Detective Kling?'

'I have not seen Detective Kling since ten years now,' Baal said.

'Oh, you all at once remember him, huh?' Ollie said.

'I remember him now, yes. But if something happened to him on Sunday night, or to his wife, as you seem to be suggesting, I can tell you without hesitation that I was with a very close female acquaintance of mine on Sunday night, and we went to a movie together.'

'Who is this very close female acquaintance?' Ollie asked.

'Her name is Henrietta Leineweber.'

'And I suppose she'll confirm that you were with her,' Carella said.

'I am sure she will confirm it,' Baal said, and nodded.

At ten minutes past three they took Baal down to the muster desk and booked him for violation of Section 265.05 of the Penal Law, a Class D felony punishable by three to seven years' imprisonment. They would have loved nothing better than to have booked him for attempted robbery. In fact, had they been patient an instant longer in the liquor store, Baal *might* have pulled the gun and said in his accented English, 'This is a stickup.' But they hadn't been expecting a robbery and had only wanted to question him about where he'd been on Sunday night, and so they'd missed out on the best kind of bust, the unexpected arrest. Even before they called Henrietta Leineweber, they knew that Baal had had nothing to do with Augusta's abduction. But they went through the routine, anyway, and of course Miss Leineweber ascertained that she and Baal had been together on Sunday night, and that was that. They were happy to be sending Baal back to jail because there was no doubt at all in their minds that he'd have robbed the liquor store that afternoon if they hadn't been on the premises waiting to talk to him. They were only sorry they couldn't be sending him back for a longer period of time.

At a quarter past three that afternoon, Manfred Baal was escorted to a detention cell in the basement of the building, to await transportation to the Criminal Courts Building downtown. By that time Augusta had worked all three pins out of their hinges, and was struggling to lift the storage-room door out of its frame.

twelve

She stepped out of the storage room into a narrow corridor painted white. She turned to her left and walked into a kitchen similarly painted white, its single window slanting wintry sunlight onto the white vinyl-tile floor. There was a swinging door at the opposite end of the kitchen, just to the right of the refrigerator, and she walked to that now, and pushed it open, and that was when the sterile whiteness ended.

She almost backed away into the kitchen again.

She was inside a shrine.

The entire apartment was a shrine. Augusta was the wall-paper and Augusta was the floor covering and Augusta was the ceiling decoration and Augusta obliterated any light that ordinarily might have filtered through the windows because Augusta covered all the windows as well. It was impossible to look anywhere without seeing Augusta. Standing there in the corridor just outside the kitchen door, she felt as though she were being reflected by thousands upon thousands of mirrors, tiny mirrors and large ones, mirrors that threw back images in colour or in black and white, mirrors that caught her in action or in repose. The corridor, and the living room beyond that, and the bedroom at the far end of the hall together formed a massive collage of photographs snipped from every magazine in which she'd ever appeared, some of them going back to the very beginning of her career. She could not possibly estimate how many copies of each edition of each magazine had been purchased and scrutinized and finally cut apart to create this cubistic monument. There were photographs everywhere. Those on the walls alone would have sufficed to create an overwhelming effect, meticulously pasted up to cover every inch of space, forming an interlocking, overlapping, overflowing vertical scrapbook. But the pictures devoured the walls, and then consumed the ceilings and dripped onto the floors as well, photographs of Augusta running rampant overhead and below, and flanking her on every side. Some of the photographs were duplicates, she saw, triplicates, quad-ruplicates, so that the concept of a myriad reflecting mirrors now seemed to multiply dangerously – there were mirrors reflecting other mirrors and Augusta stood in the midst of this visual reverberating photographic chamber and suddenly doubted her own reality, suddenly wondered whether she herself, standing there at the centre of an Augusta-echoing-Augusta universe, was not simply an echo of another Augusta somewhere on the walls. The entire display had been shel-lacked, and the artificial illumination in the apartment cast a glow onto the shiny surfaces, pinpoint pricks of light seeming to brighten a photographed eye as she moved past it, hair as dead as the paper upon which it was printed suddenly seeming to shimmer with life.

There was a king-sized bed in the bedroom. It was covered with white sheets; there were white pillowcases on the pillows. A white lacquered dresser was against one wall, and a chair covered with white vinyl stood against the adjoining wall. There was no other furniture in the bedroom. Just the bed, the dresser, and the chair – stark and white against the photo-graphs that rampaged across the floor and up the walls and over the ceiling.

She wondered suddenly what time it was.

She had lost all track of time while working on the door, but she surmised it was a little past noon now. She went quickly to the front door, ascertained that the lock on it was a key-operated deadbolt, and then went immediately into the kitchen. The unadorned white of the room came as a cool oasis in a blazing desert. She was moving toward the wall telephone when she saw the clock above the refrigerator. The time came as a shock, as chilling as the touch of the scalpel had been on her throat. She could not possibly imagine the hours having gone by that swiftly, and yet the hands of the clock told her it was now three twenty-five ... was it possible the clock had stopped? But no, she could hear it humming on the wall, could see the minute hand moving almost imperceptibly as she stared at it. The clock was working; it was three twenty-five and he'd told her he would return at three-thirty.

She immediately lifted the telephone receiver from the hook, waited for a dial tone, and then jiggled the bar impatiently when she got none. She put the phone on the hook again, lifted it again, listened for a dial tone again, and got one just as she heard the lock turning in the front door. She dropped the phone, reached for the latch over the kitchen window, and discovered at once that the window was painted shut.

She turned, moved swiftly to the kitchen table, pulled a chair from under it, lifted the chair, and was swinging it toward the window when she heard his footsteps coming through the apartment. The glass shattered, exploding into the shaftway and cascading in shards to the interior courtyard below. He was running through the apartment now. She remembered his admonition about screaming, remembered that it made him violent. But he was running through the apartment toward her, and he had promised her a wedding ceremony, and a nuptial consummation, and a slit throat – and at the moment she couldn't thing of anything more violent than a slit throat.

She screamed.

He was in the kitchen now. She did not see his face until he pulled her from the window and twisted her toward him and slapped her with all the force of his arm and shoulder behind the blow. His face was distorted, the blue eyes wide and staring, the mouth hanging open. He kept striking her repeatedly as she screamed, the blows becoming more and more fierce until she feared he would break her jaw or her cheekbones. She cut off a scream just as it was bubbling onto her lips, strangled it, but he kept striking her, his arm flailing as though he were no longer conscious of its action, the hand swinging to collide with her face, and then returning to catch her backhanded just as she reeled away from the earlier blow. 'Stop,' she said, 'please,' scarcely daring to give voice to the words lest they infuriate him further and cause him to lose control completely. She tried to cover her face with her hands, but he yanked first one hand away and then the other, and he kept striking her till she felt she would lose consciousness if he hit her one more time. But she did not faint, she sank deliberately to the floor instead, breaking the pattern of his blows, crouching on all fours with her head bent, gasping for breath. He pulled her to her feet immediately, but he did not strike her again. Instead, he dragged her out of the kitchen and across the corridor into the living room, where he hurled her angrily onto the floor again. Her lip was beginning to swell from the repeated blows. She touched her mouth to see if it was bleeding. Standing in the doorway, he watched her calmly now, and took off his overcoat, and placed it neatly over the arm of the sofa. There was only one light burning in the room, a standing floor lamp that cast faint illumination on the shellacked pictures that covered the walls, the ceiling, and the floor. Augusta lay on her own photographs like a protectively coloured jungle creature hoping to fade out against a sympathetic background.

'This was to be a surprise,' he said. 'You spoiled the surprise.'

He made no mention of the fact that she had broken the window and screamed for help. As she had done earlier, she insisted now on bringing him back to reality. 'You'd better let me go,' she said. 'While there's still time. This may be the goddamned city, but someone's *sure* to have heard—'

'I wanted to be with you when you saw it for the first time. Do you like what I've done?'

'Somebody's going to report those screams to the police, and they'll come busting in here—'

'I'm sorry I struck you,' he said. 'I warned you about screaming, though. It truly does make me violent.'

'Do you understand what I'm saying?'

'Yes, you're saying someone will have heard you.'

'Yes, and they'll come looking for this apartment, and once they find you—'

'Well, it doesn't matter,' he said.

'What do you mean?'

'The ceremony will be brief. By the time they locate the apartment, we'll have finished.'

'They'll find it sooner than you think,' Augusta said. 'The kitchen window is broken. They'll look for a broken window, and once they locate it on the outside of the building—'

'*Who*, Augusta?'

'Whoever heard me screaming. There's a building right across the way, I saw windows on the wall there ...'

'Yes, it used to be a hat factory. And, until recently, an artist was living there. But he moved out six months ago. The loft has been empty since.'

'You're lying to me.'

'No.'

'You want me to think no one heard me.'

'Someone *may* have heard you, Augusta, it's quite possible. But it doesn't really matter. As I say, it will be quite some time before we're found, even if you *were* heard. Augusta, do you like what I have done with your photographs? This didn't just happen overnight, you know, I've been working on it for quite some time. Do you like it?'

'Why did you do all this?' she asked.

'Because I love you,' he said simply.

'Then let me go.'

'No.'

'Please. *Please* let me go. I promise I won't—'

'No, Augusta, that's impossible. Really, it's quite impossible. We mustn't even discuss it. Besides, it's almost time for the ceremony, and if someone heard you screaming, as you pointed out—'

'If you really love me ...'

'Ah, but I do.'

'Then let me go.'

'Why? So you can go back to him? No, Augusta. Come now. It's time for your bath.'

'I don't *want* a bath.'

'The article about you—'

'The hell with the article about me!'

'It said you bathed twice daily. You haven't had a bath since I brought you here, Augusta.'

'I don't want a goddamn bath!'

'Don't you feel dirty, Augusta?'

'No.'

'You must bathe, anyway.'

'Leave me alone.'

'You must be clean for the ceremony. Get up, Augusta.'

'No.'

'Get off the floor.'

'Go fuck yourself,' she said.

The scalpel appeared suddenly in his hand. He smiled.

'Go ahead, use it,' she said. 'You're going to kill me, anyway, so what's the difference—?'

'If I use it now,' he said, 'it will not be pleasant. I prefer not to use it in anger, Augusta. Believe me, if you provoke me further, I can make it very painful for you. I love you, Augusta, don't force me to hurt you.'

They stared at each other across the length of the room.

'Please believe me,' he said.

'But *however* you kill me—'

'I do not wish to talk about killing you.'

'You said you were going to kill me.'

'Yes. I do not want to talk about it.'

'Why? Why are you going to kill me?'

'To punish you.'

'Punish me? I thought you loved me.'

'I do love you.'

'Then why do you want to punish me?'

'For what you did.'

'What did I do?'

'This is pointless. You are angering me. You should not have screamed. You frightened me.'

'When?'

'When? Just now. When I came into the apartment. You were screaming. You frightened me. I thought someone—'

'Yes, what did you think?'

'I thought someone had got in here and was ... was trying to harm you.'

'But you your*self* are going to harm me.'

'No,' he said, and shook his head.

'You're going to kill me. You said you're—'

'I want to bathe you now,' he said. 'Come.' He held out his left hand. In the right hand he was holding the scalpel. 'Come, Augusta.'

She took his hand, and he helped her to her feet. As they went through the apartment to the bathroom, she thought she should not have broken the window, she should not have screamed, she should not have done either of those things. The only thing to do with this man was humour him, listen to everything he said, nod, smile pleasantly, agree with him, tell him how nice it was to be in an apartment papered with pictures of herself. Stall for time, wait for Bert to get a line on him, because surely they were working on it right this minute. Wait it out, that was all. Patience. Forbearance. They'd be here eventually. She knew them well enough to know they'd be here.

'I could so easily hurt you,' he said.

She did not answer him. Calm and easy, she thought. Cool. Wait it out. Humour him.

'It is so easy to hurt someone,' he said. 'Did I tell you my mother was killed by an intruder?'

'Yes.'

'That was a long time ago, of course. Come, we must bathe you, Augusta.'

In the bathroom, he poured bubble bath into the tub, and she watched the bubbles foaming up, and heard him behind her, tapping the blade of the scalpel against the edge of the sink.

'Do you know why I bought the bubble bath?' he asked.

'Yes, because of the magazine article.'

'Is it true that you like bubble baths?'

'Yes.'

'I am going to bathe you now,' he said.

She suffered his hands upon her.

thirteen

'Now that Baal is clean so far as this job that is concerning us,' Ollie said, 'I'd like to move ahead on this other approach I've been working on.'

'Which approach is that?' Carella asked warily.

'I don't know how much experience you've had with witnesses—'

'Well, just a little,' Carella said.

'—but I've had plenty of experience with them over the years,' Ollie said, completely missing Carella's tone, 'and I'd like to tell you one thing I learned.'

'What's that?' Carella asked. Ollie was beginning to rankle. Sooner or later, Ollie *always* began to rankle. That's because Ollie was bigotted, slovenly, opinionated, crude, insensitive, gross, humourless, unimaginative ... no, that wasn't true. Ollie *was* imaginative.

'You've got to *help* witnesses,' he said.

'Help them?' Carella said. 'What do you mean?'

'This fellow Bill Bailey Won't You Please Come Home,' Ollie said.

'What about him?'

'He's the only witness we've got. He saw a truck parked out there in the service courtyard, am I right? Isn't that what he told you?'

'That's right,' Carella said.

'Okay. Now, that is all we have to go on, Steve-a-reeno,' he said, and Carella winced. 'We have got an old fart of a man who says he saw a white truck through a greasy window. That is right here in your report, m'friend, right here for one and all to see, ah, yes.' Carella winced again; if anything, Ollie was even *more* obnoxious when he was imitating W. C. Fields. 'It also says in your report,' Ollie said, falling back into his natural voice, and tapping the typed sheets with his forefinger, 'that old Bill Bailey Won't You Please Come Home doesn't know what *kind* of truck it was, all he knows is it was a *white* truck. That is not much to go on, Steve-a-reeno. There must be hundreds of different kinds of white trucks in this city, am I right?'

'Right,' Carella said. 'Yes, right. Right.'

'Which is where old Bill Bailey Won't You Please Come Home needs a little help.'

'Ollie, I wish you wouldn't do that each time you mention the man.'

'Do what?' Ollie asked.

'Repeat the whole title of the song. It's not necessary to do that each time you mention the man's name. Let's just call him Bill Bailey, okay? Because, to tell the truth, it's beginning to rankle, your giving the full title of the song each time you mention—'

'You've got to keep calm,' Ollie said pleasantly. 'Steve, you and the rest of the fellows up here are very nice guys, I mean that sincerely. But you ain't thinking too clearly on this case, as witness the fact you haven't given old Bill Bailey Won't You Please Come Home any help. That's because you're all very close to Bert Kling, I can understand that. But you can't allow that to muddle up your thinking, Steve. I mean that sincerely. Which is why it's a good thing I'm on the case with you. We need a clear head around here. What I'm saying, Steve, is somebody's got to keep this thing in perspective, and I guess that's me.'

'I guess so,' Carella said, and sighed.

'How many different kinds of white trucks did you say were in the city?'

'I didn't say,' Carella said.

'How many *would* you say?' Ollie asked.

'I have no idea.'

'Guess.'

'Ollie . . .'

'What time did I leave here this afternoon, would you remember that?' Ollie asked.

'Ollie, I wish you wouldn't talk to me as if I were a suspect being interrogated,' Carella said. 'If you have something to say,

I wish you'd just say it straight out, instead of asking me leading questions designed to—'

'You mean to tell me you don't remember what time I left here this afternoon?'

'It must've been about three-thirty,' Carella said, and sighed again.

'That's right. Do you know where I went?'

'Where did you go?'

'I went to Ainsley Avenue, the stretch of Ainsley Avenue where all the automobile showrooms are. It took me ten minutes to get there. I went into each and every one of those showrooms, and that took me another twenty minutes, and then it took me ten minutes to get back here ...'

'Ollie, I don't need a timetable.'

'Do you know *why* I went to those showrooms, Steve?'

'Why?'

'To get *these*,' Ollie said, and lifted his dispatch case from the floor, and placed it in the centre of Carella's desk. 'Now I'm going to tell you without further ado, m'friend, what is in this dispatch case here on the desk before me,' Ollie said. 'What's in this little case here is a rare collection of folders, ah, yes, containing photographs of every type of truck and van made by the major American and foreign automobile manufacturers, yes, indeed. I have dozens and dozens of different pictures in this little dispatch case. Do you know what I am going to do with those pictures, m'boy?'

'I can guess,' Carella said.

'I am going to show them to old Bill Bailey Won't You Please Come Home,' Ollie said.

Alexander Pike had some pictures, too.

He came up to the squadroom at 4:17 p.m., exactly three minutes after Ollie had gone out to talk to old Bill Bailey Won't You Please Come Home. Carella had casually mentioned to him that Bailey didn't get to work till ten each night, but Ollie quickly reported that he had already called the R & M Luncheonette (which name he had got from Carella's report, ah, yes), and they'd given him Bailey's home address. Now Pike was here in the squadroom. And Pike had some pictures too.

'I still had a roll in the camera,' he said. 'I put it in on Sunday night, and forgot it was in there, and I didn't use that particular camera again till this morning. I shot the rest of the roll this morning. Do you understand what I'm saying so far?'

'Yes,' Carella said.

'And this afternoon I developed the roll. Because what I shot this morning was for a job, you understand. And I had to make some contacts, so I could—'

'Yes, I understand,' Carella said.

'Well, the *first* picture on the roll, the one I'd forgotten was still in the camera, was a picture Kling took on Sunday night.'

'*Kling* took it?'

'Yes. I asked him to take it. It's a picture of me and Augusta.'

'I see,' Carella said patiently.

'It was taken in the hotel lobby.'

'Um-huh.'

'Just inside the revolving doors.'

'Yes, um-huh.'

'There was a fifty-millimetre lens on the camera, and Kling was shooting with the strobe light. That's what gave the depth of field and focus. Otherwise everything behind me and Augusta might have been in darkness.'

'I see, yes,' Carella said, nodding.

'Well, I was looking at the contacts with a magnifying glass, really trying to second-guess the ones the editor would pick, when I saw the picture Kling had taken. The one of me and Augusta. Oh, he was maybe three feet away from us when he took the picture. And just behind us, coming through the revolving doors in the background, there's a man. Strobe lit him beautifully, you can see him as plain as day. He looked familiar, Mr Carella. So I made an enlargement of the picture, and it's the same man, all right.'

'What man?'

'The one who was sitting in church watching the wedding. The man with the blonde hair and the light eyes.'

'May I see the enlargement, please?' Carella said.

'Certainly,' Pike said, and unclasped a manilla envelope, and took from it an eight-by-ten black-and-white glossy, which he placed before Carella on the desk. The photograph showed a beaming Pike and Augusta in the foreground. In the background, apparently having just come through the revolving doors, was the unidentified blond man. The photograph had caught him turning away from the camera, his hand coming up toward his face, as though to shield it.

'That's him, all right,' Carella said.

'See his hand there?' Pike said. 'There's a ring on it. In all those pictures I took inside the church, his hands were folded in his lap, and the ring wasn't visible. In fact, his *hands* weren't even visible except in the two pictures I shot across him toward the centre aisle, and that was from the left, so the right hand couldn't be seen, there was just both hands clasped on that dark overcoat, with the left hand facing the lens. Do you remember the pictures I mean?'

'Yes, I do.'

'But the ring *is* visible in this picture Kling took, and I figured there'd be no harm blowing it up, so I started zeroing in on it, and I finally brought it up as big as I could without losing definition. The one I did after this one is all grainy, you can't tell anything from it. But this one is pretty good.' He reached into the manilla envelope and put another eight-by-ten glossy on the desk. 'Your eyes are probably sharper than mine,' he said, 'and even *I* can read what's on that ring.'

Carella looked at the photograph. It was a remarkably clear enlargement of what was unmistakably a graduation ring. The stone in the centre of the ring was multifaceted, light in tone, possibly an amethyst. It was set into the massive body of the ring, and the circle surrounding the stone was stamped with the words RAMSEY UNIVERSITY.

'That's right here in the city, isn't it?' Pike said.

'Yes,' Carella said briefly, and glanced up at the clock. It was almost four-thirty. Without another word to Pike, he pulled the telephone directory to him.

Old Bill Bailey Won't You Please Come Home looked even older than Ollie thought he would. The minute Ollie laid eyes on him, in fact, he doubted Bailey would be of any assistance at all; one look at those cheaters told him the man was blind as a bat. He showed his shield, anyway, and introduced himself and asked if he could come into the apartment. The apartment smelled of cat shit, which was strange, since there weren't any cats in evidence anywhere around.

'Detective Carella tells me you saw a white truck in the hotel's service courtyard late Sunday night ...'

'That's right,' Bailey said.

'What I'm here for right now, Mr Bailey, is to see if I can't help you identify that truck for us.'

'Well, I already told the other detective ... What'd you say his name was?'

'Carella.'

'Carella, that's right, I already told him I didn't know what kind of truck it was.'

'Well, it so happens, Mr Bailey,' Ollie said, unclasping his dispatch case, 'that I've got several pictures of trucks here, trucks of different sizes and shapes, and I wonder if you might take a look at them and see if any of them ring a bell. See if we can't zero *in* on the kind of truck it might have been, okay?'

'Okay.'

'These are folders from all the automobile companies, we'll just leaf through them, okay? See if we can't spot the kind of truck you saw on Sunday night.'

'Okay,' Bailey said.

'Okay, fine,' Ollie said. 'Let's start with these right here, this is the whole line of Ford pickup trucks. These two on the cover, did the truck you saw—'

'No, it didn't look anything like those,' Bailey said.

'In what way was it different?'

'Well, it didn't have an open back. It just wasn't that kind of a truck.'

'No cargo box, you mean?'

'That space in the back there.'

'That's right, the cargo box.'

'That's right, it didn't have one of those.'

'Well, okay then,' Ollie said, 'let's put aside the pickups and take a look at some of these other folders. Now, I'm just assuming, Mr Bailey, that it wasn't a big trailer truck in that alley there.'

'No, no, nothing as big as a trailer truck.'

'Okay, let's take a look at this Chevy folder here, the one marked "Bus Chassis".'

'It wasn't a bus,' Bailey said.

'Well, I realize it wasn't a *school* bus like this yellow one on the cover ...'

'It wasn't a bus at *all*.'

'But you see, there are these smaller ones inside,' Ollie said. 'This one they call the Suburban, that seats nine kids ...'

'No, it was bigger than that.'

'How about this one here, this Sportvan that seats twelve?'

'No, it was bigger than that, too.'

'Are we moving in the right direction, though? Was it a *kind* of van? Is that the *type* of truck it was? What you would call a van?'

'Well, it wasn't a pickup truck, that's for sure. It was a truck closed all around.'

'Like a van.'

'If that's what you want to call it,' Bailey said.

'Well, that's what the companies call them, you see. The automobile companies. They call them vans.' Ollie picked up another folder. 'See this here? It says "Dodge Tradesman Vans" on the cover. Now, that's the kind of thing I'm talking about. Was it something like this?'

'Something like it, but not quite.'

'Did it have a sliding door on the side?'

'I only saw the back.'

'Here's another picture inside here. It has this rear door, too, see it? Did the one you saw have a door on the back?'

'I think so.'

'But you're not sure.'

'It was white, I'm sure of that. And it was bigger than that.'

'Bigger than this van here, huh?'

'Yes.'

'But it *was* a van, huh? The type of thing we're talking about . . .'

'Yes, I think it was a van.'

'Good, we're getting there. I've got plenty of folders here, just take your time, Mr Bailey, because what we want to do is get a bead on—'

'I *am* taking my time,' Bailey said.

'Good, good,' Ollie said. 'Now, here's a folder with what Ford calls "Econoline Vans". You said the truck was white – well, here's a picture inside here of a white parcel-delivery van. Did the one you saw look anything like this?'

'No,' Bailey said.

'Well, how about this?' Ollie said. 'This book with the Chevy Step-Vans in it. Here's a white one right on the cover. How about it?'

'No,' Bailey said.

'Lots of milk and bakery trucks look like this,' Ollie said. 'You told Detective Carella that it might've been a milk truck, or a bakery truck . . .'

'Or a linen truck. I thought it might've been delivering linens or something.'

'Linen trucks look like this, too,' Ollie said.

'Yeah, but the truck I saw in the alley wasn't that one.'

'How about this one on the next page here? This looks like a bigger van than the one on the cover.'

'No, the one I saw wasn't that big.'

'Okay, let's keep turning. Here's a smaller one.'

'The orange one, you mean?'

'Yes.'

'The truck I saw was white.'

'I know, forget the colour for a minute. We're going for size and body type.'

'No, it didn't look like that,' Bailey said.

'But it was a Step-Van?'

'I don't know. I'm not sure.'

'Well, look at these,' Ollie said, turning to the last page in the folder. 'These pictures show how the Chevy Step-Vans can be equipped. Here's one for a company that sells fire-prevention gear, here's one—'

'There,' Bailey said. 'That's what it looked like.'

'This one?'

'The other one. Right there on the bottom of the page. It looked something like that.'

'Here?' Ollie said, and pointed to the photograph.

'That's the one,' Bailey said.

They were looking at a picture of a white van with red lights just above the windshield, and red lights mounted on the hood. A red stripe ran completely around the centre of the van, and lettered onto this stripe in white, on the hood and sides of the van, was the word EMERGENCY. The copy to the left of the photograph read: *Step-Van King equipped with electronic life-support equipment found in most hospital emergency rooms. Can handle four litter patients.*

'A goddamn ambulance,' Ollie said.

There were six buttons on the bodice of the gown, spaced between the square neckline and the Empire waist. The gown was made of cotton, with rows and rows of tucked white lace, and more lace on the cuffs of the full sleeves. A silk-illusion veil crowned Augusta's auburn hair, and she was carrying a small bouquet of red roses. He had dressed her himself, fumbling with the delicate lace edged panties and bra, sliding the lacy blue garter up over her left thigh, adjusting the veil on her head, and then presenting her with the bouquet. He led her barefooted into the living room now, and asked her to sit on the sofa, facing him. She sat, and he told her to clasp both hands around the shaft of the bouquet, and to hold the flowers on her lap and to look straight ahead of her, neither

to the right nor to the left, but straight ahead. He was standing directly in front of her, some six feet away, as he began
his recitation.

'We are witnesses here,' he said, 'the two of us alone, we
are witnesses to this holy sacrament, we are witnesses. You
and I, man and woman, and child asleep in innocence, we are
witnesses. We are witnesses to the act, we have seen, we have
seen. I have seen her before, yes, I have witnessed her before,
I have seen photographs, yes, she knew this, she was a famous
model, there would be roses at the door, roses from strangers,
they would often arrive without warning. I have seen photographs of her, yes, she was quite famous. I have seen her
dressing, too, I have sometimes witnessed – the bedroom door
ajar, I have sometimes in her underthings, yes, she was quite
beautiful, I have witnessed, but never naked, never that way,
das Blut, ach!'

He shook his head. Though Augusta knew no German,
she instantly understood the word '*Blut*.' He repeated the
word in English now, still shaking his head, his eyes on the
roses in Augusta's lap.

'Blood. So much blood. Everywhere. On the floor, on her
legs, *nackt und offen*, do you understand? My own mother,
meine Mutter. To expose herself that way, but ah, it was so
very long ago, we must forget, *nein*? And in fairness, she was
dead, you know, he had cut her throat, you know, forgive
them their trespasses, they know not what they do. So much
blood, though ... so much. He had cut her so bad, yes, even
before her throat, she was so ... so many cuts ... she ...
everywhere she had touched, there was blood. Running away
from him, you know. Touching the walls, and the bureau, and
the closet door, and the chairs, blood everywhere. Screaming,
Ach, ach, I covered my ears with my hands, *Bitte, bitte*, she
kept screaming again and again, Please, please, *Bitte, bitte*,
where is my father to let this happen to her, where? There
is blood everywhere I look. Her legs are open wide when I
go into the bedroom, there is blood on the insides of her
legs, shameless, like a cheap whore, to let him *do* this to her?
Why did she allow it, *why*? Always so careful with *me*, of

course, always so modest and chaste – Now, now, Klaus, you must not stay in the bedroom when I am dressing, you must not peek at your mother, eh? Run along now, run along, there's a good boy – petticoats and lace, and once in her bloomers, with nothing on top, smelling of perfume, I wanted so much to touch you that day, Augusta, but of course I am too small – you are too small, Augusta, your breasts. You are really quite a disappointment to me, I don't know why I bother loving you at all, when you give yourself so freely to another. Ah, well, it was a long time ago, *nein*? Forgive and forget, let bygones be bygones, we are here today to change all that, we are here today as witnesses.'

He smiled abruptly, and looked up from the roses, directly into Augusta's face.

'Johanna, my love,' he said, 'we are here to be married to-day, you and I, we are here to celebrate our wedding. We are here to sanctify our union that will be, we are here to witness and to obliterate. The other, I mean. Your union with another, we will obliterate that, Johanna, we will forget that shameless performance – why did you let him *do* it?' he shouted, and then immediately said, 'Forgive me, Augusta,' and walked to where she was sitting on the sofa, and took the bouquet from her hands and placed it on the floor. Then, kneeling before her, he took both her hands between his own, and said, simply, 'I take you for my wife, I take you for my own.'

He kissed her hands then, first one and then the other, and rose, and gently lifted her from the couch and led her into the bedroom.

The president of Ramsey University was a man in his late sixties. He had come to the school from a college in Boston, and had been presiding there only since the beginning of September. He would not in any case have recognized the photographs Carella showed him, but he looked at them politely, and then shook his head, and suggested that Carella go through the back issues of the school's yearbook. He buzzed for his secretary, and she led Carella into the school library, where copies of the yearbook went all the way back to the year the school was founded.

'Is this a murder case or something?' the secretary asked. She was a pert blonde in her middle twenties, wearing a skirt Carella would have thought somewhat brief for the halls of academe.

'No, it's not a murder case,' he said.

'What is it then?'

'Just a routine investigation,' he said.

'Oh,' she said obviously disappointed. 'I thought it might be something exciting.' She shrugged elaborately, and then clicked across the length of the library on her high heels, leaving Carella alone in the echoing room.

His job would have been simpler had he known the man's exact age, but of course he did not. Judging from the photographs, they had estimated his age at somewhere between twenty-five and thirty years old. Twenty-two is the average age at which students in America are graduated from college, and there are usually two graduating classes – one in January, and the other in June. Carella did not want to waste time. He took the outside age estimate – thirty years – and subtracted twenty-two from it, and came up with eight. That was where he would start, with the yearbooks published eight years ago. He found them on the shelves the president's secretary had earlier indicated, and he pulled down both the January and June issues. Beginning with the January issue, he leafed slowly through the pages, aware that eight years ago the man might have looked markedly different, and not wanting to miss him in his eagerness for a positive make. He found no one resembling the man in either the January or the June yearbooks. Patiently, he began working his way upward through the succeeding years.

He knew that he might possibly have to wade through sixteen yearbooks in all – two issues a year for the eight years spanning the possible graduation dates for a man who was now anywhere between the ages of twenty-five and thirty. Carella was prepared to scrutinize all sixteen of those yearbooks, and if he found nothing in any of them, he was prepared to look at *every* damn yearbook on those shelves. But as it turned out, he did not have to spend more than a half-hour in the school library.

The man's name was Klaus Scheiner. He had been graduated six years ago, which put his present age at twenty-eight; their original estimate hadn't been a bad one, after all. He had been a member of the Glee Club and the Honour Society, had been elected to Phi Beta Kappa in his junior year, and had been president of the German Club. As was the custom in some college yearbooks, a couplet followed the strict listing of Scheiner's undergraduate achievement. The couplet read:

Klaus is groovy, Klaus is cool,
Klaus is going to medical school

The scalpel was in his hand.

He had tried to make love to her, and had failed, and now he rose from the bed angrily, and said, 'Put on your underthings! Are you a whore? Is that what you are?' and watched as she lifted the long bridal gown and put on the white lace-edged panties, the only garment he had earlier asked her to remove.

'You do not have to answer,' he said. 'I *know* what you are, I have known for a long time.'

She said nothing.

'I suppose you are disappointed in me,' he said. 'Someone like you, who knows so many men. I suppose my performance was less than satisfying.'

Still, she said nothing.

'Have you known others like me?' he asked. 'In your experience, have you known others who could not perform?'

'I want you to let me go,' she said.

'Answer me! Have you known others like me?'

'Please let me go. Give me the key to the front door, and—'

'I'm sure you have known a great many men who had medical problems such as mine. This is entirely a medical problem, I will see a doctor one day, he will prescribe a pill, it will vanish. I myself was almost a doctor, did you know that? I was Phi Beta Kappa at Ramsey University, did you know that? Yes. I was an undergraduate there, Phi Beta Kappa. And I was accepted at one of the finest medical schools in the country. Yes. I went for two years to medical school. Would you like to know what happened? Would you like to know why I am not a doctor today? I could have been a doctor, you know.'

'I want to leave here,' she said. 'Please give me the key.'

'Augusta, you are being absurd,' he said. 'You cannot leave. You will *never* leave. I am going to kill you, Augusta.'

'Why?'

'I told you why. Would you like to know what happened in medical school, Augusta? Would you like to know why I was expelled? I mutilated a cadaver,' he said. 'I mutilated a female cadaver. With a scalpel.'

They knew he had gone to medical school from Ramsey U, and they knew the vehicle parked in the service courtyard of the hotel had been an ambulance. So first they went through the city's five telephone directories looking for a listing for a Dr Klaus Scheiner.

There were no Klaus Scheiners in any of the directories.

So they looked up at the clock on the squadroom wall, and they manned the squadroom telephones, and began calling each and every hospital in the city. There were a lot of hospitals, but they all had to be called because the man Klaus Scheiner had gone to medical school, and he had been driving an ambuance on the night of the abduction. Assuming he worked at one of the hospitals, there would be an address on file for him. That's all they wanted or needed: his address. Once they got that, *if* they got that, they would break in on him. But getting that address, *if* it existed, *if* he indeed worked at one of the hospitals, meant making telephone calls. And making telephone calls took time.

Kling made none of the calls.

'Hello,' Willis said into the telephone, 'this is Detective Willis of the 87th Squad, we're trying to locate ...'

'A man named Klaus Scheiner,' Meyer said into the telephone. 'He may be a ...'

'Doctor,' O'Brien said, 'or perhaps he's ...'

'Connected in some other way with the hospital,' Carella said.

'That's Scheiner,' Parker said. 'I'll spell it for you. S ... C ...'

'H ... E ...' Delgado said.

'I ... N ...' Hawes said.

'E ... R,' Ollie said.

Kling paced, and listened, and watched.

And waited.

She backed away from him.

He was coming for her with the scalpel in his hand. He was between her and the doorway. The bed was in the centre of the room, she backed toward it, and then climbed onto the mattress, and stood in the middle of the bed, ready to leap to the floor on the side opposite whichever one he approached.

'I urge you not to do this,' he said.

She did not answer. She watched him, waiting for his move, poised to leap. She would use the bed as a wall between them. If he approached it from the side closest to the door, the right-hand side, she would jump off onto the floor on the left. If he crawled onto the bed in an attempt to cross it, she would run around the end of it to the other side. She would keep the bed between them forever if she had to, use it as a barrier and a—

He thrust the scalpel at her, and seemed about to reach across the bed, and she jumped to the floor away from him, and realized too late that his move had been a feint. He was coming around the side of the bed, it was too late for her to manoeuvre her way to the door, she backed into the corner as he came toward her.

She would remember always the sound of the door being kicked in, would remember too the swift shock of recognition that darted into his eyes and the way his head turned sharply away from her. She could see past him to the front door, could see the bolt shattering inwards, and Steve Carella bursting into the room, a very fat man behind him, and then Bert –

and the scalpel came up, the scalpel came toward her.

They were all holding guns, but the fat man was the only one who fired. Steve and Bert, they just stood there looking into the room, they saw the scalpel in his hand, they saw her in a wedding gown, crouched in the corner of the room, the scalpel coming toward her face – *I mutilated a female cadaver* – the fat man taking in the situation at once, his gun coming level, and two explosions erupting from the muzzle.

She would realize later that the fat man was the only one who did not love her. And she would vow never to ask either Steve or Bert why they had not fired instantly, why they had left it to Fat Ollie Weeks to pump two slugs into the man who was about to slit her throat.

Weeks	We just told you your rights, and you just told us you understood your rights and didn't need no lawyer here to tell us what this whole thing is about. Now, I just want you to understand one more thing, you shithead, and that's you're in no danger of dying, the doctor says you're gonna be fine. So I don't want no trouble later, I want it clear on the record when we get to court that nobody said you were going to die or anything. We didn't get you to make a statement by saying you were a dying man or nothing like that.
Scheiner	That's true.
Weeks	So that's why the stenographer's taking all this down if you want to tell us about it.
Scheiner	What do you want to know?
Weeks	Why'd you kidnap the lady?
Scheiner	Because I love her.
Weeks	You love her, huh? You were ready to f'Christ sake *kill* her when we—
Scheiner	*And* myself.
Weeks	You were going to kill yourself, too?
Scheiner	Yes.
Weeks	Why?
Scheiner	With her dead, what would be the sense of living?

Weeks	You're crazier'n a fuckin bedbug, you know that? *You*'re the one was gonna kill her.
Scheiner	To punish her for what she did.
Weeks	What'd she do?
Scheiner	She allowed him.
Weeks	She allowed him, huh? You fuckin lunatic, you're a fuckin lunatic, you know that? How'd you know what hotel they were at?
Scheiner	I followed them from the church.
Weeks	Were you at the reception?
Scheiner	No. I waited downstairs for them.
Weeks	All the while the reception was going on?
Scheiner	Yes. Except for when I moved the ambulance.
Weeks	When was that?
Scheiner	About eleven o'clock, I think it was. I moved it into the alley behind the hotel. That was after I learned where the service courtyard was.
Weeks	Then what?
Scheiner	Then I came around to the front again – because the alley door was locked, I couldn't get in that way. And I was just coming through the revolving doors when I saw them standing there, just inside the doors – he was taking a picture of her and another man. I turned away, I walked toward the phone booths.
Weeks	How'd you find out what room they were in?
Scheiner	I picked up a house phone in the lobby, and asked.
Weeks	You see that? You see what they'll tell you? You walk in any hotel in this city, you ask them what room Mr So-and-so is in, they'll tell you. Unless he's a celebrity. How'd you get into the room, Scheiner?
Scheiner	I used a slat from a Venetian blind.
Weeks	How come you know how to do that? What *are* you, a burglar?
Scheiner	No, no. I drive an ambulance.
Weeks	Then how'd you learn about that?
Scheiner	I have read books.

Weeks	And you learned how to loid a door, huh?
Scheiner	I learned how to force a door, to push back the bolt.
Weeks	That's loiding.
Scheiner	I don't know what you call it.
Weeks	But you know how to *do* it pretty good, don't you, you shithead? Didn't you know there was a *cop* in that room. He could've blown your head off the minute you opened the door.
Scheiner	I did not think he would have a gun on his wedding day. Besides, I was prepared.
Weeks	For what?
Scheiner	To kill him.
Weeks	Why?
Scheiner	For taking her from me.

They put Kling and Augusta into a taxi, and then they went out for hamburgers and coffee. Fat Ollie Weeks ate six hamburgers. He did not say a word all the while he was eating. He had finished his six hamburgers and three cups of coffee before Meyer and Carella finished what they had ordered, and then he sat back against the red leatherette booth, and belched, and said, 'That man was a fuckin lunatic. I'da cracked the case earlier if only we hadn't been dealing with a lunatic. Lunatics are very hard to fathom.' He belched again. 'I'll bet old Augusta ain't gonna forget *this* for a while, huh?'

'I guess not,' Meyer said.

'I wonder if he got in her pants,' Ollie said.

'Ollie,' Carella said very softly, 'if I were you, I wouldn't ever again wonder anything like that aloud. *Ever*, Ollie. You understand me?'

'Oh sure,' Ollie said.

'*Ever*,' Carella said.

'Yeah, yeah, relax already, will ya?' Ollie said. 'I think I'll have another hamburger. You guys feel like another hamburger?'

'Are you sure you understand me?' Carella asked.

'Yeah, yeah,' Ollie said. He called the waitress over, and

ordered another hamburger, and then was silent until the hamburger came. He gulped it down without saying a word, and then he wiped the back of his hand across his mouth and said, completely out of the blue, 'I think I'll apply for a transfer to the Eight-Seven. I mean it, that's one hell of a precinct you got there. That's just what I'm gonna do.'

Carella looked at Meyer.

'Yep,' Ollie said.

Ed McBain
Blood Relatives £2.50

Saturday night, and party night on the Precinct – the perfect
backdrop for a knife-carrying sex attacker. Seventeen-year-old
Muriel was stabbed to death and her cousin Patricia got away with a
slashed cheek. When she ran into the station house Kling watched
the bloody hand-prints appear on the glass panel. A messy start to a
case that got messier – every time Patricia changed her story . . .

'Totally gripping . . . he rivets the reader throughout'
JILL NEVILLE, BBC KALEIDOSCOPE

The McBain Brief £2.50

Twenty stories from the man who created the 87th Precinct. Stories
of the street and the city, stories of the cops and their prey. Life in a
Chinese lobster-shop, the making of a porn queen, and the agony of
being jailed with a non-stop talking cellmate. Places and people only
he can describe.

Calypso £2.50

What a lousy way to die. Calypso King George Chadderton,
murdered on a wet September street in the 87th Precinct. Brains
spattered on a sidewalk on a wet city night is something detectives
Carella and Meyer can do without. And then Clara Hawkins, a leggy
black hooker, ends up the same way. Carella and Meyer figure the
connection between some tall, crazy killer with a Smith & Wesson
and a weird lady in black living on an island with a caged-up man
and an alsatian . . .

'Gothic hair-raiser . . . leaves the reader twitching' GUARDIAN

Dick Francis
Blood Sport £2.99

'Instantly readable . . . attempted murders on the Thames and on the ranch, death in the Blue Grass country of Kentucky, three stallions hi-jacked, blackmail, burglary and bugging devices from dashboard to powder room' THE SPORTING LIFE

Banker £3.50

'Dick Francis is off at a gallop again! *Banker* is about £5 million of horseflesh called Sandcastle, a sort of super-Arkle. A young trainer gets a merchant bank to invest in him, and merchant banks, like all banks, only invest in sure things . . .' DAILY MAIL

'Strongly told . . . this must be his best yet'
THE TIMES LITERARY SUPPLEMENT

Bonecrack £2.99

'This time it's a rich monomaniac who will stop at nothing, not blackmail, not murder, to ensure his son will be a crack Derby jockey. A classic entry with a fine turn of speed'
EVENING STANDARD

All Pan books are available at your local bookshop or newsagent, or can be ordered direct from the publisher. Indicate the number of copies required and fill in the form below.

Send to: **CS Department, Pan Books Ltd., P.O. Box 40,**
             Basingstoke, Hants.   RG21 2YT.

or phone: 0256 469551 (Ansaphone), quoting title, author
             and Credit Card number.

Please enclose a remittance* to the value of the cover price plus: 60p for the first book plus 30p per copy for each additional book ordered to a maximum charge of £2.40 to cover postage and packing.

*Payment may be made in sterling by UK personal cheque, postal order, sterling draft or international money order, made payable to Pan Books Ltd.

Alternatively by Barclaycard/Access:

Card No. | | | | | | | | | | | | | | | |

Signature:

Applicable only in the UK and Republic of Ireland.

While every effort is made to keep prices low, it is sometimes necessary to increase prices at short notice. Pan Books reserve the right to show on covers and charge new retail prices which may differ from those advertised in the text or elsewhere.

NAME AND ADDRESS IN BLOCK LETTERS PLEASE:

....

Name ————————————————————————

Address ————————————————————————

————————————————————————

————————————————————————

————————————————————————

3/87